LIGHTNING DRAW

Buck West knew what was coming when the card-player stood up and said, "I think you're a coward, mister."

Buck slowly placed the shot glass of whiskey down on the rough bar and eyeballed the man. Two guns worn low and tied down. The leather hammer thongs off. "I'll tell you what I think," he said. "I think you don't know a bunghole from your mouth."

The man flushed and his dirty hands hovered over his guns. "I think I'll jist kill you for that."

"Bet or fold," Buck said.

The man's hands dipped down. Buck's right-hand .44 roared. The gunhand was dead before he hit the floor.

In the silence that followed the bartender was the first to speak, his voice hushed and awe-filled:

"I never even seen the draw!"

RETURN OF THE MOUNTAIN MAN

BY WILLIAM W. JOHNSTONE

ZEBRA BOOKS
KENSINGTON PUBLISHING CORP.

ZEBRA BOOKS

are published by

Kensington Publishing Corp.
475 Park Avenue South
New York, NY 10016

Second printing: May 1987

Printed in the United States of America

This book is pure Western fiction. Any resemblance to actual living persons is purely coincidental. To the best of my knowledge there is no town in Idaho called Bury.

To my friend who answers my endless questions concerning weapons of the old west: Hollis Erwin.

Back of the bar, in a solo game, sat Dangerous Dan McGrew, And watching his luck was his light-o'-love, the lady that's known as Lou.

—Robert W. Service

1

The man called Smoke looked at the new wanted poster tacked to a tree. This one had his likeness on it. He smiled as he looked at the shoulder-length hair and the clean-shaven face on the poster. The artist had done a dandy job.

But it in no way resembled the man who now called himself Buck West.

Kirby Jensen had been sixteen years old when the old mountain man called Preacher hung the nick-name Smoke on him. Preacher had predicted that Smoke would turn out to be a very famous man. And he had. As one of the most feared gunfighters in all the west.

It was not a reputation Smoke had wanted or sought.

Smoke now wore his hair short-cropped. A neat, well-trimmed beard covered his face. He no longer wore one pistol in cross-draw fashion, butt-forward. He now wore his twin .44s butt back and the holsters tied down low. He was just as fast as before. And that was akin to lightning.

He had turned his Appaloosa, Seven, loose in a valley several hundred miles to the east. A valley so lovely it was nearly impossible to describe.

Nicole would have loved it.

Seven had gone dancing and prancing off, once more running wild and free.

Nicole.

9

He shook his head and pushed the face of his dead wife from his mind. He turned his unreadable, cold, emotionless brown eyes to the west. The midnight-black stallion he now rode stood steady under his weight. The man now called Buck stood six feet, two inches, barefooted. He weighed one eighty: all hard-packed muscle and bone. His waist was lean and his short hair ash-blond.

The stallion shook his head. Buck patted him on the neck. The stallion quieted immediately. The animal's eyes were a curious yellow/green, a vicious combination that vaguely resembled a wolf's eyes. The stallion had killed its previous owner when the man had tried to beat him with a board. Smoke had bought the horse from the man's widow, gentled him, and learned to respect the animal's feelings and moods.

The stallion's name was Drifter.

Smoke had carefully hidden his buckskins, caching them with his saddle and other meager possessions in the valley where the Appaloosa, Seven, now grazed and ran free with his brood of mares.

Smoke had very carefully pushed all thoughts of the past behind him. He had spent months mentally conditioning himself not to think of himself as the gunfighter Smoke. His name was now Buck. Last names were not terribly important in the newly opened western frontier, and it had been with a smile that Buck chose West as his last name.

Buck West. Smoke was gone—for a time.

Buck laughed. But it was more a dark bark, totally void of humor.

Drifter swung his head around, looking at the man through cold killer eyes. Buck's packhorses continued to graze.

High above, an eagle soared, pushing and gliding

toward the west. Buck could have sworn that it was the same eagle he had seen months back, after the terrible shoot-out at the silver camp not far from the Uncompahgre. At least fourteen men had died under his guns that smoky, bloody day. And he had taken more than his share of lead, as well. It had taken him months to fully recover.

Many months back, in the southwestern corner of Wyoming, he had seen the first wanted poster.

WANTED
DEAD OR ALIVE
THE OUTLAW AND MURDERER
SMOKE JENSEN
10,000.00 REWARD
CONTACT THE SHERIFF AT BURY, IDAHO TERRITORY

He had removed the wanted poster and tucked it in his shirt pocket. He knew he would see many, many more of the dodgers as he made his way west. He had looked up to watch an eagle soar high above him, gliding majestically northwestward.

He had said, with the big skies and grandeur of the open country as witnesses, "Take a message with you, eagle. Tell Potter and Richards and Stratton and all their gunhands that I'm coming to kill them. For my pa, for Preacher, for my son, and for making me an outlaw. And if I can do it, they'll die twice as hard as Nicole died. You tell them, eagle. Tell them I'm coming after them."

The eagle had circled, dipped its wings, and flown on.

Buck shook away the memories, clearing his head of things dead and buried and gone. He let the smoldering coals of revenge burn on, deep within his soul. He would fan the coals into white-hot flames

11

when branding time arrived. And he would do the branding—with hot lead.

The man who had earned the reputation as one of the most feared gunfighters in the newly opened west spoke gently to Drifter and the big cat-footed stallion moved out through the timber.

Buck was just west of the Rockies, skirting south of the Gros Ventre Range. He would—unless he hit some sort of snag—make Moose Flat in two days. Once at the Flat, he would camp for a few days and rest Drifter. Then he would ride for Bury, Idaho Territory.

Bury was a good name, Buck thought. For that is exactly what I intend to do to Stratton and Richards and Potter: bury them!

It was cool during the day and flat-out cold at night; early spring when Buck crossed the still ill-defined line into Idaho Territory. He had seen several bands of Indians, but they had left him alone. He knew they'd seen him, for this was their country, and they knew it as intimately as the roots of a tree knows the earth that nurtures it. But Indians, as Preacher had once put it, were notional critters.

Buck moved out, slowly. He would take his time, get accustomed to the country, and eyeball everything in sight. For if he made it out of Bury alive, he was going to need more than one back door and one hell of a good hiding place.

Buck wore gray pin-striped trousers tucked into soft calfskin boots. Black shirt. His hat was black, low-crowned, and wide-brimmed. His leather vest was black. His belt was silver-studded with a heavy buckle. A jacket and slicker were tied behind the saddle, over the saddlebags. A Henry repeating rifle rested in a boot, butt forward instead of the usual fashion of the butt facing back. He did not ride in the usual slump-shouldered manner of the old mountain men, but instead sat his saddle ramrod straight, cavalry fashion. Because of this, many who saw the handsome, cold-eyed young man believed him to be ex-cavalry. He let them think it, knowing that helped to further disguise his past.

He carried a two-shot derringer in his left boot, in his right boot a long-bladed, double-edged dagger—that knife in addition to the Bowie he wore on his gunbelt, behind his left-hand gun.

Buck was an expert with all the weapons he carried. The legend growing around the man stated there was no faster gunhand in all the west. He was faster than the Texas gun Hardin; even more steel-nerved than Wild Bill; meaner than Curly Bill; when he was in the right, crueler than any Apache; as relentless in a hunt as any man who ever lived.

The old mountain man, Preacher, who helped raise him from a lad, had taught him fistfighting and boxing and Indian wrestling. But even more importantly, Preacher had taught him how to win, teaching him that it don't make a good gawddamn how you win—just win.

The old mountain man had said, and the boy had remembered, "Long as you right, Smoke, it don't make no difference how you win. Just be sure you in the right."

And Lord God, how fast the young man was with those deadly .44s.

Buck gave Drifter his head, letting the horse pick his own way at his own pace, staying close to the timber, away from open places, always edging slightly south and west. He wanted to enter the mostly uncharted center of the Territory from the south. Just north of the Craters of the Moon, Buck would turn

Drifter's nose north until he hit the Big Lost River. He would follow that through some of the most beautiful and wild country in the Territory. He would then track the Big Lost for a time, then head more north than west until reaching the new town of Challis. There, he would resupply and head north, following the Salmon River for about thirty-five miles. Bury was located about midway between the Salmon and the town of Tendoy.

But if Buck had his way, the town of Bury would soon cease to exist.

It would be several more years before the toll road would be started between Challis, reaching to Bonanza, with a spur to Salmon. Only then would the big-scale silver mining at Bay Horse get underway.

But that was future. This was now. And Buck was not heading for Bury to pan for gold, search for silver, or start a ranch. And he really didn't care all that much if he died doing what he'd set out to do—just so long as he got it done. The men now living and prospering in and around Bury had directly killed his brother. They had ordered out the men who had killed his father; raped, tortured, and murdered Buck's wife, Nicole; killed his baby son; and killed his best friend and mentor, the old mountain man, Preacher.

And then they had done their cruel best to kill the man who now called himself Buck West.

Stratton, Potter, and Richards had thrown their best gunhands at the young man. He had killed them all.

Thus far, Stratton, Potter, and Richards had failed to stop Buck.

Buck had no intention of failing.

2

Buck was being followed. He had yet to catch a glimpse of his pursuers, but he knew someone was tracking him; knew it by that itchy feeling between his shoulder blades. Twice in as many days he had stopped and spent several hours checking his back-trail. But to no avail. Whoever or whatever it was coming along behind him was laying way back, several miles at least. And they were very good at tracking. They would have to be, for Buck not to have spotted them, and Preacher had taught the young man well.

Puzzled, Buck rode on, pushing himself and his horses, skirting the fast growing towns in the eastern part of the state, staying to the north of them. Because of the man, or men, tracking him, Buck changed his plans and direction. He rode seemingly aimlessly, first heading straight north, then cutting south into the Bridger Wilderness. He crossed into Idaho Territory and made camp on the north end of Grays Lake. He was running very low on supplies, but living off the land was second nature to Buck, and doing without was merely a part of staying alive in a yet wild and untamed land.

The person or persons following him stayed back, seemingly content to have the young man in sight,

15

electing not to make an appearance—yet.

Midafternoon of his second day at Grays Lake, Buck watched Drifter's ears prick up, the eyes growing cautious as the stallion lifted his head.

Buck knew company was coming.

A voice helloed the camp.

"If you're friendly, come on in," Buck called. "If you want trouble, I'll give you all you can handle."

Buck knew the grizzled old man slowly riding toward his small fire, but could not immediately put a name to him. The man—anywhere between sixty-five and a hundred and five—dismounted and helped himself to coffee and pan bread and venison. He ate slowly, his eyes appraising Buck without expression. Finally, he belched politely and wiped his hands on greasy buckskins. He poured another cup of coffee and settled back on the ground.

"Don't talk none yet," the old man said. "Jist listen. You be the pup Preacher taken under his wing some years back. Knowed it was you. Ante's been upped some on your head, boy. Nearabouts thirty thousand dollars on you, now. You must have a hundred men after you. Hard men, boy. Most of 'em. You good, boy, but you ain't that good. Sooner 'er later, you'll slip up, git tared, have to rest, then they'll git you." He paused to gnaw on another piece of pan bread.

"The point of all this is? . . ." Buck said.

"Tole you to hush up and listen. Jawin' makes me hungry. 'Mong other things. Makes my mouth hurt too. You got anything to ease the pain?"

"Pint in that pack right over there." Buck jerked his head.

The old mountain man took two huge swallows of the rye, coughed, and returned to the fire. "Gawd-damn farmers and such run us old boys toward the

16

west. Trappin's fair, but they ain't no market to speak of. Ten of us got us a camp just south of Castle Peak, in the Sawtooth. Gittin' plumb borin'. We figured on headin' north in about a week." He lifted his old eyes. "Up toward Bury. We gonna take our time. Ain't no point in gettin' in no lather." He got to his feet and walked toward his horses. "Might see you up there, boy. Thanks for the grub."

"What are you called?" Buck asked.

"Tenneysee," the old man said without looking back. He mounted up and slowly rode back in the direction he'd come.

"You're not any better lookin' than the last time I saw you!" Buck called to the old man's back, grinning as he spoke.

"Ain't supposed to be," Tenneysee called. "Now git et and git gone. You got trouble on your backtrail."

"Yeah, I know!" Buck shouted.

"Worser'n Preacher!" Tenneysee called. "Cain't tell neither of you nuttin'!"

Then he was gone into the timber.

Fifteen minutes later, Buck had saddled Drifter, cinched down the packs on his pack animal, and was gone, riding northwest.

He wondered how many men were trailing him. And how good they were.

He figured he would soon find out.

Staying below the crest of a hill, Buck ground-reined Drifter and scanned his backtrail. It was then he caught the first glimpse of those following him. Four riders, riding easy and seemingly confident. He removed a brass spyglass from his saddlebags and pulled it fully extended, sighting the riders in. He did not recognize any of them, but could see they were all heavily armed. Hardcases, every one of them.

Buck looked back over his shoulder, toward the

17

west. He smiled at the sight. Blackfeet. And the way they were traveling, the gunhands and the warlike Blackfeet would soon come face to face.

The Blackfeet had not always hated the white man. Long before the Lewis and Clark expedition, the Blackfeet had been in contact with the French-Canadian trappers of the Hudson's Bay Company. For the most part, they had gotten along. But in 1806, when the Lewis and Clark expedition split up, Clark turning southward to explore the Yellowstone River, Lewis taking the Blackfoot Branch as the best route to the Missouri, Lewis had encountered a band of Blackfeet. No one knows who started the fight, or why, and the journals of Lewis don't say, but the battle had a long-lasting effect. Since the Blackfeet were the most powerful and warlike tribe in the Northwest, their hatred following the battle closed both rivers to American travel.

Buck was puzzled why so many Blackfeet were in this part of the Territory, somewhat off their beaten path. He concluded, after looking them over through his spyglass, that they were a war party, and had been quite successful, judging from the scalps on their rifles and coup sticks and wound into their horses' manes.

Buck smiled as the Blackfeet spotted the white men first. Within seconds, the Blackfeet had vanished, the war party splitting up, lying in silent wait to spring the deadly ambush.

Buck didn't wait around to see the fun. He quickly mounted up and took off in the other direction. Blackfeet had a reputation for being downright testy at times.

And from the north, a pair of old eyes watched as Buck rode out. The eyes followed the young man until he was out of sight.

Buck heard the shots from the short battle as he

continued to put more distance between himself and the Blackfeet. The old man waited almost an hour before leaving his hiding place. Leading a pack animal, he slowly rode after Buck. He was in no hurry, for he knew where Buck was going and what he was going to do. He just wanted to be there to help the young man out.

1874 in most of Idaho Territory was no place for the faint-hearted, the lazy, the coward, or the shirker. 1874 Idaho Territory was pure frontier, as wild and woolly as the individual wanted to make it. It would be three more long, bloody, and heartbreaking years for the Nez Percé Indians before Chief Joseph would lead his demoralized tribe on the thirteen-hundred mile retreat to Canada. There, the chief would utter, "I am tired; my heart is sick and sad. From where the sun now stands I will fight no more forever."

But in 1874, the Indians were still fighting all over Idaho Territory, including the Bannocks and Shoshones. It was a time for wary watchfulness.

It had been fourteen years since an expedition led by Captain Elias D. Pierce of California had discovered gold on Orofino Creek, a tributary of the Clearwater River. It wasn't much gold, but it was gold. Thousands had heard the cry and the tug of easy riches, and thousands had come. They had poured into the state, expecting to find nuggets lying everywhere. Many had never been heard from again. As Buck rode through the southern part of the state, heading for the black and barren lava fields called the Craters of the Moon, even here he was able to see the mute heartbreak of the gold-seekers: the mining equipment lying abandoned and rusting, the dredges in dry creek beds. Now, in early summer, a time when the creeks and rivers were starting to recede, Buck spotted along the banks a miner's boot, a pan. He wondered what stories they could tell.

He rode on, always checking his backtrail. He had a vague uneasy feeling that he was still being followed. But he could never spot his follower. And that was cause for alarm, for Buck, even though still a young man, was an expert in surviving in the wilderness.

He skirted south of the still-unnamed village of Idaho Falls, a place one man claimed "openly wore the worst side out."

Buck rode slowly but steadily, coming up on the south side of the Big Lost, north of the Craters of the Moon. He stopped at a trading post at what would someday become a resort town called Arco. Inside the dark, dirty place, filled with skins and the smell of rotgut whiskey, Buck bought bacon and beans and coffee from a scar-faced clerk. The clerk smelled as bad as his store.

Buck's eyes flicked over several wanted posters tacked to the wall. There he was.

"Last one of them I seen had ten thousand dollars reward on it," he said, to no one in particular. He noticed several men at a corner table ceased their card playing.

"Ante's been upped," the clerk/bartender said with a grunt.

"Man could do a lot with thirty thousand dollars," Buck said. He walked to the bar and ordered whiskey. He didn't really care for the stuff but he wanted information, and bartenders seldom talked to a nondrinking loafer. "The good stuff," he told the bartender. The man replaced one bottle and reached under the counter for another bottle.

He grinned, exposing blackened stubs of teeth. "This one ain't got no snake heads in it."

Buck lifted the glass. Smelled like bear piss. Keeping his expression noncommittal, he sipped the whiskey. Tasted even worse.

"Have any trouble coming from the east?" the bartender asked.

"How'd you know I come from the east?"

"That's the way you rode in."

"Seen some Blackfeet two-three days ago. But they didn't see me. I didn't hang around long."

"Smart."

"You see four men, riding together?" the voice came from behind Buck, from the card table.

"Yeah. And so did the Blackfeet."

"Crap! You reckon the Injuns got 'em?"

"I reckon so. I didn't hang around to see."

"You mean you jist rode off without lendin' a hand?"

"One more wouldn't have made any difference," Buck said quietly, knowing what was coming.

"Then I reckon that makes you a coward, don't it?" the cardplayer said, standing up.

Buck slowly placed the shot glass of bear piss back on the rough bar. He eyeballed the man. Two guns worn low and tied down. The leather hammer thongs off. "Either that or careful."

"You know what I think, Slick? I think it makes you yellow."

"Well, I'll tell you what I think," Buck said. "I think you don't know your bunghole from your mouth."

The man flushed in the dim light of the trading post. His dirty hands hovered over his guns. "I think I'll jist kill you for that."

"Bet or fold," Buck said.

The man's hands dipped down. Buck's right-hand .44 roared. The gunhand was dead before he hit the

21

floor, the slug taking him in the center of the chest, exploding his heart.

"I never even seen the draw," the bartender said, his voice hushed and awe-filled.

"Any of you other boys want to ante up in this game?" Buck asked.

None did.

The dead man broke wind as escaping gas left his cooling body.

"He were my partner," a man still seated at the table said. "But he were in the wrong this time. I lay claim to his pockets."

"Suits me," Buck said. No one had even seen him holster his .44. "He have a name?"

"Big Jack. From up Montana way. Never spoke no last name. Who you be?"

"Buck West. I been trackin' that damned Smoke Jensen for the better part of six months."

Big Jack's partner visibly relaxed. "Us, too. I would ask if you wanted some company, but you look like you ride alone."

"That's right."

"Name's Jerry. This here's Carl and Paul. Don't reckon you'd give us a hand diggin' the hole for Jack?"

"I don't reckon so."

"Cain't much blame you."

"Bury him out back," the bartender said. "Deep. If he smells any worser dead than alive I'll have to move my place of business."

3

The men watched as Buck rode away, ramrod straight in the saddle. Jerry said, "That young feller is faster than greased lightning."

"Faster than Jesse, I betcha!"

"Ain't no faster than Wild Bill, though," Paul said.

Jerry spat on the ground. "Wild Bill ain't crap!"

"You don't say!" Carl turned on his friend. "I suppose you gonna tell us Wild Bill didn't clean up Abilene?"

"He sure as hell didn't. I know. I were there. Me and Phil Coe. I seen Wild Bill shoot him with a pair of derringers after Phil done put his gun away. Then he turned around and shot the marshal, Mike Williams. Wild Bill better not ever try to brace that there Buck West. Buck's a bad one, boys. Cold-eyed as a snake."

It would be almost exactly two and one half years later, on the afternoon of August 2, 1876, in Deadwood, South Dakota, when a cross-eyed, busted-nose wino named Jack McCall would blow out Hickok's brains as he studied his poker hand of Aces and Eights. Wild Bill would be thirty-nine years old.

"I think Potter ought to know about this here Buck West," Jerry said. "Think I'll take me a ride later on. Let Buck get good and gone."

"We'll tag along."

Late that afternoon a stranger rode up to the trading post and walked inside. He cradled a Henry repeating rifle in the crook of his left arm. "I seen the fresh grave out back," he said to the barkeep. "Friend of yourn?"

"Hell, no! Don't git me to lyin'."

"Man ought to have a marker on his grave, don't you think?"

"I'll git around to it one of these days. Maybe. Big Jack was all they called him."

"Better than nothin'. I don't reckon he died of natural causes?"

"Not likely. You gonna talk all day or buy a drink of whiskey?"

The buckskin-dressed old man tossed some change on the wide rough board that passed for a counter. "That buy a jug?"

"And then some. No, sir. That Big Jack fancied hisself a gunhand, I guess." He placed a dirty cup and a clay jug of rotgut on the counter. "But he done run up on a ringtailed-tooter this day. Feller by the name of Buck West. You heard of him?"

"Seems I have, somewheres. Bounty hunter, I think. But he's a bad man to mess with."

"Tell me! Why, he drew so fast a feller couldn't even see the blur! Big Jack's hand could just touch the butt of his .36 when the lead hit him in the center of the chest. Dead 'fore he hit the ground."

The old man smiled. "That fast, hey?"

"Lord have mercy, yes!" He eyeballed the old man. "Ain't I seen you afore? You a mountain man, ain't you? Ain't so many of you old boys left."

"Not me, podner. I'm reetared from the east. Come out here to pass my golden years amid the peace and tranquility of the High Lonesome."

The bartender, no spring chicken himself, narrowed his eyes and said, "And you jist as full of shit now as you was forty year ago, you old goat!"

The old man laughed. "Wal, you jist keep that information inside that head of yourn and off your tongue. You do that and I won't tell nobody I know where Rowdy Jake Kelly has retared to. You still got money on your head, Rowdy."

"Man, I heard you got kilt last year! Shot all to hell and gone over to Needle Mountains."

"Part of it's true. I got all dressed up in my finest buckskins, rode an old nag up into the hills, and laid me down to die. Lordy, but I was hurtin' some. Longer I laid there the madder I got. I finally got up, said to hell with this, and rode off. Found me one of my Injun kids—or grandkids, I ain't real sure which—and she took care of me. You keep hush about this, now, you hear?"

"I never saw you afore this day," Rowdy Jake Kelly said.

The old man nodded, picked up his jug of whiskey, and rode off.

Buck had left the trading post and followed the Big Lost River north. He pushed his horses, rested them, then pushed them hard again, putting as many miles as possible between himself and the trading post. He had a hunch the men back at the trading post would be hell-bent for Bury. They were bounty hunters; he knew from the look. He smiled grimly at what they might think if they knew they had been within touching distance of the man called Smoke.

Buck found himself a hidden vantage point where he could watch the trail, and settled in for the evening. He built a hand-sized fire and fixed bacon and beans

25

and coffee. Using tinder-dry wood, the fire was virtually smokeless. He kept his coffee warm over the coals.

Just at dusk, he heard the sounds of riders. Three riders. He watched as they passed his hiding place at a slow canter, heading north, toward the trading post at Mackay. He watched and listened until the sounds of steel-shod hooves faded into the settling dusk. Using his saddle for a pillow, Buck went to sleep.

Just as the first rays of dawn streaked the horizon, Buck was fording the Big Lost, heading for the eastern banks and the Lost River Range. He did not want to travel those flats that stretched for miles before reaching Challis, preferring to remain in the timber.

He wanted to take his time getting to Bury for two reasons: One, he wanted the story of the shoot-out at the trading post to reach the right ears—namely Potter, Stratton, and Richards. Men like that could always use another gun, and Buck intended to be that other gun. Two, he still had that nagging sensation of being followed. And it annoyed him. He knew, *felt*, someone was back there. He just didn't know who.

The eighty-mile ride from the trading post to Challis passed slowly, and Buck took his time, enjoying the sights of new country. Buck was a man who loved the wilderness, loved its great beauty, loved the feeling of being alone, although he knew perfectly well he certainly was not alone. There were the eagles and hawks who soared and glided above him. The playful camp-robber birds, the squirrels and bears and puma, the breathless beauty of wild flowers in early summer. No, he was not alone in the wilderness. Alone was just a state of mind. Buck had only to look around him for company, compliments of nature.

Sensing more than hearing movement, Buck cut

toward the west and into the deep timber of the Lost River Range. He quieted his horses and waited in the timber. Then he spotted them. It was a war party, and a big one. From this distance—he couldn't risk using his spyglass, for it was afternoon and he was facing west, and didn't want to risk sunlight bouncing off the lense—he could only guess the tribe. Nez Percé, Bannock—maybe Sheepeater. Preacher had told him about the little known but highly feared Sheepeaters.

Buck counted the braves. Thirty of them, all painted up and looking for trouble. He cursed under his breath as they reined up and dismounted, after sending lookouts in all directions.

Were they going to make camp? Buck didn't know. But he knew it was awfully early for that.

To the south, Borah Peak, almost thirteen thousand feet high, loomed up stark in the high lonesome. The highest peak in the state, Borah dominated matters for miles.

Buck sat it out for several hours, watching and waiting out the long minutes. The horses seemed to sense the urgency of the moment and were very quiet. Occasionally, Buck would slip back to them to pat and water them, whispering gently to the animals, keeping them still and calm.

Returning from his last trip to the animals, Buck looked out over the valley he was high above. He grunted, not in surprise, but rather a "I should have known" grunt.

The Indians were gone, having left as swiftly and silently as they had come. Buck lay still for another ten minutes, mulling the situation over in his mind.

The war party had built no fires, either cook or signal. They had met with no other Indians. Why had they stopped: Buck had no idea. But he knew one thing: he damn sure wasn't going to head out after

27

them. Whichever direction the war party had taken, he planned to head in the other direction. And he did. Before two minutes had passed, Buck had tightened cinches and was heading out. He found where the war party had ridden south, so he swung Drifter's head and pointed his nose north, toward the muddy, brawling town of Challis, located just to the northwest of the Salmon River. Buck would hang around Challis for a few days, listening to the miners talk and attempting to get the feel of what the townspeople thought of Bury, some thirty-five miles north and slightly east.

Challis was one short business street, more saloons than anything else, with tents and shacks and a few permanent-looking homes to the north. Most of the shacks appeared to have been tossed in their location by some giant crap-shooter.

Buck stabled his horses—he wasn't worried about anyone stealing Drifter, for the stallion would kill anyone who entered his stall—and taking his Henry repeating rifle, a change of clothing, and his saddle-bags, Buck walked toward the town's hotel.

After checking in, Buck went to a barber shop and took a hot bath, a young Chinese man keeping the water hot with additional buckets of water. After Buck had soaped off the weeks of dirt and fleas, he dressed in dark trousers, white shirt, and vest. He left his boots to be shined and settled in the barber chair.

"Short," he told the barber. "And trim my beard."

"Passin' through?" the barber asked.

"Could be. Mostly just drifting."

The barber had noted Buck's tied-down guns. Being an observant man, and one raised on the frontier, he knew a fast gun when he saw one. And this man sitting in his chair was a gunhand, and no tinhorn. The butts of his .44s were worn smooth from handling, with no marks in the wood to signify kills. Only a tinhorn did that, and tinhorns didn't last long in the west.

But there was something else about this young man. Confidence. That was it. And a cold air about him. Not unfriendly, just cold.

"If it's silver you're huntin' "—he knew it wasn't—"big strike north and east of here. Close to the Lemhi River."

"Not for me," Buck told him. "Too much work involved in that."

"Uh-huh. You be handy with them .44s?"

"Some folks say that."

"You head north from here, follow the Salmon until the river cuts through the Lemhi Range, then head east. You'll come up on the town of Bury."

"Hell of a name for a town."

"It's right proper, considerin' the size of their boot hill. You'll see."

"Why would I want to go to someplace called Bury?"

"Maybe you don't. Then again, you might find work up there."

"Might do that. How's the law in this town?" Buck set the stage with that question.

"Tough when they have to be. Long as it's a fair fight, they won't bother you."

"I never shot no one in the back," Buck replied, putting it just a bit testily.

"You don't have that look about you, that's for sure." The barber's voice was very bland.

"Where's the best place to eat?"

"Marie's. Just up the street. Beef and beans and apple pie. Good portions, too. Reasonable."

They weren't just good portions; they were huge. The food simple but well-prepared. The apple pie was delicious. Buck pushed the empty plate away and settled back, leaning back in his chair, his back to a wall. He lingered over a third cup of coffee and watched the activity in the street through the window.

He was waiting for the marshal or sheriff to make his appearance. It didn't take long.

The town marshal entered the cafe, a deputy behind him. The deputy held a sawed-off double-barrel twelve-gauge express gun in his hands. And it appeared he had used it before.

The marshall was not a man to back up or mince words. He sat down at Buck's table, facing him, and ordered a cup of coffee. He stared at Buck.

Buck returned the stare.

"Passin' through?" the marshal asked.

"Might stay two or three days. I'm in no big hurry to get anywhere."

"You got a name?"

Buck smiled. "I'm not wanted."

"That don't answer my question."

"Buck West." Buck then placed the man. Dooley. He'd been a lawman over in Colorado for years. A straight, no-nonsense lawman. But a fair one.

Dooley pointed up the street. "Them houses with paint on them beginning at the end of the street is off-boundaries for drifters. Decent folks live there. The dosshouses is on the other end of the street." He pointed. "Thataway." He jerked his thumb. "The road out of town is thataway. Feel free to take it as soon as possible."

"I don't intend to cause you or your men any trouble, Marshal," Buck said softly.

"But you will," the marshal replied just as softly. "You just got that air about you."

"You're a very suspicious man, Marshal."

"Goes with the job, son." The marshal drained his

coffee cup, stood up, and started to leave. He looked once more at Buck. "You sure look familiar, mister."

"I just have a friendly face," Buck said solemnly.

"Yeah," the marshal said drily. "I'm sure that's it."

4

As he stood facing the two men in the saloon, it occurred to Buck that perhaps the marshal just might have been right. Buck had entered the saloon, ordered a beer, and had nursed it for about fifteen minutes before the cowboy with a loud and arrogant mouth had begun needling him.

"You gonna drink that beer or stand there and look at it with your face hangin' out?"

Buck ignored him.

"Boy, you better talk to me!" the cowhand said.

"I intend to drink this beer," Buck said, "in my own good time. Not that it's any of your business."

The cowboy took a step backward, a puzzled look on his face. Buck knew the type. He was big and broad and solid with muscle. And he was used to getting his way. He had been a bully all his life. He belittled anything he was too stupid to comprehend—which was nearly everything.

"That's Harry Carson, stranger," the barkeep whispered.

"Is that supposed to mean something to me?" Buck said, not bothering to keep his voice to a whisper.

"And his buddy is Wade Phillips," the barkeep plunged ahead.

"I wonder if either one of them can spell unimpressed," Buck said. He felt the old familiar rage fill him. He had never been able to tolerate bullies; not even as a boy back in Missouri.

The deputy who had been with Marshal Dooley earlier that day leaned against the bar, silently watching the show unfold before him. Carson and Phillips were both loud-mouthed troublemakers. But he felt he had pegged this tall young man right. If he was correct in his assumption, Carson and Phillips would never pick another fight after this night.

The deputy slipped out of the line of possible gunfire and sipped his beer.

"What'd you say, buddy?" Carson stuck his chin out belligerently.

Buck fought back his anger. "Go on, Carson. Back off, drink your drink, and leave me be."

"You got a smart mouth, buddy." Phillips stuck his ugly, broad-nosed and boozy face into it.

Upon entering the place, Buck had slipped the hammer thongs off his .44s. He slowly turned to face the twin loudmouths.

"I'm saying now I'm not looking for trouble. But if I'm pushed into it, so be it."

"Talks fancy, don't he?" Phillips's laugh was ugly. But so was he, so it rounded out.

"Yeah," Carson said. "And got them fancy guns on, too. But I betcha he ain't got the sand in him to duke it out."

Buck's smile was faint. He had pegged the men accurately. Both men probably realized that neither one of them could beat Buck in a gunfight, so they would push him into a fight with fists and boots. And if he didn't fight them at their own game, he would be branded a coward.

The bully's way.

Buck took off his gunbelt and laid it on the bar. Spotting the deputy, he slid the hardware down the bar to him. "Look after those, will you, please?"

"Be glad to, West. Watch 'em. They're both dirty at the game."

Buck drained his beer mug and said, "Not nearly as dirty as I am."

Then Buck smashed the mug into Carson's face. The heavy mug broke the man's nose on impact. Buck then jabbed the jagged broken edges into the man's cheek and lips, sending the bully screaming and bleeding to the sawdust covered floor.

Buck hit Phillips a combination left and right, glazing the man's eyes with the short, brutal punches. Buck did not like to fight with his bare fists, knowing it was a fool's game. But sometimes that was the only immediate option. Until other objects could be brought into play.

Phillips jumped to his boots, in a crouch. Buck stepped close and brought one knee up, at the same time bringing both hands down. As his hands grabbed the man's neck, his knee came in contact with the man's face. The crunch of breaking bones was loud in the saloon.

The fight was over. Carson lay squalling and bleeding on the floor beside the unconscious Phillips. Buck turned around. Marshal Dooley was standing by his deputy.

"Any law against a fair fight, Marshal?" Buck asked. "It was two against one."

"And they were outnumbered at those odds," Dooley said. "No, West, there is no law against it. Yet," he added. "But someday there will be."

Buck retrieved his guns and buckled them around his waist. "Not as long as there are people so stupid as to place and praise physical brawn over the capacity of

34

reason."

Dooley blinked. "Who are you, West? You're no drifting gunhand. You've got intelligence."

"Anybody who wishes to do so can read, Marshal. And most of us can think and reason. That's who I am. Good night, Marshal."

Buck picked up his hat from the bar and walked out into the night.

"More to him than meets the eyes, Marshal," the deputy observed.

"Yeah," said the marshal. "But it's that unknown about him that I'm afraid of."

Buck spent the next three days loafing and listening around Challis. He read a dozen six-month-old newspapers, bought a well-worn book of verse by Shelley and began reading that. He played a little poker, winning some, losing some, and ending up breaking about even. Twice he saw a couple of the most disreputable-looking men he'd seen in years. He knew they were mountain men, and he knew they were checking on him. The men had to be close to seventy years old, but they still looked like they could wrestle a grizzly bear. And probably win.

Some of the so-called "good people" of the community sniffed disdainfully at the sight of the buckskin-clad old men, snubbing them, having highly uncomplimentary things to say about them. Buck wanted to say, "But these men opened the way west. These men faced the dangers, most of the time alone. And many of their compadres were killed opening the way west. Had it not been for them, you folks would still be waiting to make the trek westward. These men are some of the true heroes of our time; living legends. You should welcome them, praise them, not snub and insult them."

But Buck kept his mouth shut, knowing he would be wasting his words. He recalled the words of that fellow called Thoreau: If a man does not keep pace with his companions, perhaps it is because he hears a different drummer. Let him step to the music which he hears, however measured or far away.

But Buck knew there was more to it than that. And he silently cursed his lack of education, vowing to read and retain more wisdom of words. He had left his books, his precious books, back at the cabin in that lovely lonely meadow, where he had buried his wife and son. Nicole and Arthur. He knew someday he'd return to that valley. If he lived through his mission.

He leaned back in his chair on the boardwalk, his back to a storefront, and pondered away a few moments, wondering why so many people built false and unworthy idols. These old mountain men were, in some cases, like military men. Looked down on and cursed until the need for them arises, then, as that moment passes, they are once more shunted aside. Like those signs Buck had been seeing on some stores: No Irish wanted here.

Buck's philosophical meanderings were shoved aside as his eyes found the two men walking slowly down the center of the dirt main street.

Phillips and Carson. Both of them wearing two pistols. Their hands were near the pistols, ready to draw. With a sigh, Buck stood up and looked around him. Then he remembered: Marshal Dooley and his deputy had left that morning to ride out to a ranch; something about rustling.

"Get out in the street, West!" pig-face Phillips yelled.

Buck stepped off the boardwalk, slipping the leather thongs from the hammers of his .44s as he walked.

Front doors and windows facing the street banged shut as the residents headed for cover. Gunfights were nothing new to these people. They just wanted to view it from a safe place.

"It doesn't have to be this way, boys!" Buck called. But he knew it did. With people like Carson and Phillips, winning was the only way. So-called "loss of face" was totally unacceptable. Reasoning was beyond their comprehension.

Something is wrong with this method of settling disputes, Buck thought. And something is very wrong with my own personal vendetta. But the young man, self-educated as far as his education went, knew that, at this point in the advancement of civilization, a dusty street and the smell of gunsmoke was judge and jury.

But he also knew that lawyers weren't the final answer, either. They mucked matters up too much, twisting and reshaping the truth.

There had to be a better middle ground. But damned if he knew what it was.

"You ready to die, boy?" Carson yelled.

Buck cut his eyes for just an instant. Standing in front of a saloon was one of the men from back at the trading post. What was his name? Jerry. Yeah. Big Jack's buddy. And standing a few yards from him, an old buckskin-dressed mountain man. The mountain man, old and big and still solid, cradled a Henry repeating rifle in the crook of one massive arm.

"We all have to see the elephant sometime," Buck said. He could tell the men facing him were nervous. Since he had whipped them that night, Buck had heard stories about Carson and Phillips. They were thugs and ne-er-do-wells. Shiftless troublemakers. Buck had heard that the pair had used guns before, but were not gunhands, per se. They were back-shooters, cowards. But of course, as Buck knew well, most bullies are cowards.

Buck stood in the center of the street, standing tall and straight, his big hands, rough and work-hardened, close to his guns.

There was fifty feet between the men when Carson and pig-face Phillips stopped. Buck could see the sweat on the men's face. Buck knew he could not afford to draw first. Even though the men were trash, this was their town; Buck was a stranger. They had to draw first in order for it to be called self-defense. Even if it was two on one.

Buck stood quietly, waiting.

"You had no call to scar us up like you did," Carson yelled. "You don't fight fair."

Buck waited.

Then Buck knew what had been wrong with his philosophical thinking of a few moments ago. These men were mentally ill-equipped to face the day-to-day struggles of living peacefully. But was that Buck's fault? Was he, and others like him, responsible for Carson and Phillips and others like them? What would happen if he presented them with an armload of books, saying to them, "Here, gentlemen, within these pages lie the answers. Here is a thousand years of wisdom. Understand this and you'll learn how to cope; how to live decently . . ." Buck shook those thoughts away.

We are all put here on this earth with the capability to learn to reason. These men, and others like them, don't want to learn. Therefore, it lies on their head, not mine. We come into this world naked and helpless and squalling. Yes. But we are equal to the task of learning.

Buck mentally settled it.

To hell with them!

"Ain't you got no tongue?" Phillips hollered. "Cain't you talk?"

"What do you want me to say?" Buck asked.

"Beg and we'll let you turn tail and run on out of here!" Carson yelled.

"I beg to no man," Buck's words were softly offered.

"Then die!" Phillips screamed. He reached for his gun.

Buck let him clear leather before he drew his right-hand .44. He fired twice, one slug taking Phillips in the belly, the second slug hitting the man in the center of his chest. Phillips fell backward, mortally wounded.

Carson had not drawn. The man's face was chalky white. He watched as Buck holstered his .44. Buck waited patiently.

The street was silent as a hundred pairs of eyes watched in awe and disbelief, the incredible speed of the tall young man an astonishing thing to witness. His hand had been like a blur as he drew, cocked, and fired.

"Back off, Carson," Buck said. "Just turn around and walk away and it's over. How about it?"

A hundred pairs of ears heard him offer the man his life.

A hundred pair of ears heard Carson refuse the offer. "Hell with you!" Carson snarled, and went for his gun.

Born with the gift of ambidextrousness, Buck was as fast with his left hand as with his right. In a heartbeat, Carson lay dead on the dusty street. The man's bootheels and spurs beat a death march on the dirt as his spirit joined that of Phillips, winging their way to their just rewards.

Buck reloaded his .44s and holstered them. He walked across the street to his chair and sat down.

People began streaming out of offices and stores and saloons. They gathered around the fallen pair of would-be gunhands. They looked at Buck, sitting calmly on the boardwalk.

"Mind if we get the man to take your picture?" some called.

Buck didn't mind at all. He wanted Stratton and Potter and Richards to hear of this.

The town's only photographer gathered up his bulky equipment and came on a run.

Buck sat calmly, waiting for the marshal.

5

"When you gonna tell the boy you still alive and kickin'?" Beartooth asked the mountain man who had been following Buck.

He was called Beartooth because he didn't have a tooth in his mouth. And hadn't had in forty years. No one knew what his Christian name was, and it wasn't a polite question to ask.

"I might not never," the mountain man said. "He think I'm dead. Might be best to keep it thataway. I'm only goin' in if and when he needs help."

"He'll need help," Dupre said. "Plenty guns up at Bury. And they all going to be aimed at your friend."

Dupre had drifted up from New Orleans in the late '20s. His accent was still as thick as sorghum.

"You ain't seen Smoke—'scuse me, *Buck*, git into action," the mountain man said. "He's hell on wheels, boys. Best I ever seen. And I seen 'em all."

"Don't start lyin', Preacher," Greybull said.

Greybull was a mountain of a man. It took a mule to pack him around.

"What do you think about it, Nighthawk?" Preacher asked.

"Ummm," the old Crow grunted.

"Whutever the hell that means," Tenneysee said. "Damned Injun ain't said fifteen words in the fifty year I been knowin' him."

"Ummm," Nighthawk said.

"Might make the lad feel better if'n he knowed you was still breathin'," Pugh said. Pugh was commonly referred to as "Phew!" He hated water. "Then again," Phew said. "It might make him irritable. He probably said all sorts of kind words 'bout you. An' thinkin' of enough kind words 'bout you to bury you probably took him the better part of a month."

"Phew," Preacher said. "Would you mind changin' positions just a tad. Right there. Don't move. Now the wind is right. Why don't you take a bath? Damn, you'd make a vulture puke."

"Well, if you ask me—" Audie said.

"Nobody did," Beartooth said. "Hell, nobody can *see* you."

Audie was a midget. About three and a half feet tall. And about three and a half feet wide. He was a large amount of trouble in a very compact package.

"As I was saying," Audie said, "before your rudeness took precedent." Audie had taught school in Pennsylvania before the wanderlust hit him and he had struck out for the west, on a Shetland pony. When the Indians had seen him, they'd laughed so hard they forgot to kill him. "I think it best that Preacher keep his anonymity for the period preceding our arrival in Bury. Should Preacher reveal his living, breathing self to the young man, it might prove so traumatic as to be detrimental to Jensen's well-being."

"Ummm," Nighthawk said, nodding his head in agreement.

"Whut the hale's far are you shakin' your head about, you dumb Injun?" Greybull said. "You don't know no more whut he said than us'ins do."

"Ummm," Nighthawk said.

"Whatever Audie said, I agree with him," Matt

said. Matt was a negro. Big and mean and one-eyed.

Matt was probably the youngest man present. And he was at least sixty-five. He had lost his eye during a fight with an angry mountain lion. Matt had finally broken the puma's back.

"Good Gawd, Audie!" Deadlead said. "Cain't you talk American? What the hell did you jist say?"

Deadlead had earned his nickname from being a crack shot with a pistol. Like most of the mountain men, no one knew what his Christian name was.

"Ummm," Nighthawk said.

"I say we break camp and meander on up towards Bury," Powder Pete said. "Old as we is, some of us might not make the trip if we wait much longer."

"I opt fer that myself," Tenneysee said. "What do you say, Nighthawk?"

"Ummm."

"I'll not have this town filled up with would-be gunhands looking to make themselves a reputation," Marshal Dooley said. "Get your truck together and hit the trail, West."

"Friendly place you have here, Marshal," Buck said with a double-edged smile.

"Yes, it is," Dooley said, ignoring the sarcasm in Buck's tone. "Something about you invites trouble, boy." He waved a hand absently. "I know, I know. You didn't start the fight. And I understand from talking with witnesses you even tried—slightly—to back away from it. That's good. But not good enough. Clear out, West."

"In the morning soon enough?"

Dooley wavered. He nodded his head. "Stay out of the saloons tonight and be gone by dawn."

Buck stepped out of the office onto the boardwalk.

He didn't object to being asked to leave town. He didn't blame the law. It was time to be moving on. And there was no point in delaying his departure until morning. Buck was getting that closed-in feeling anyway. And so was Drifter. Last time he'd looked in on the animal, Drifter had rolled his eyes and tossed his head. And then proceeded to kick in the back of his stall.

Buck walked to the hotel, gathered up his gear, and headed for the stable. He had bought his supplies earlier and was ready to go.

"Ready to go, Drifter?" Buck asked the stallion.

Drifter reared up and smashed the front of his stall.

"Guess so," Buck mumbled.

The band of mountain men met Lobo at the base of Greyrock Mountain, about halfway between the Sawtooth Wilderness area and Challis. Lobo briefed the men on what he'd seen in town.

It was rumored that Lobo had once lived with wolves.

"Faster than greased lightnin'," Lobo said. "I never seen nothin' like it afore in my life. An' the lad didn't even blink an eye doin' it."

"Tole you!" Preacher said to the men, grinning.

"Don't start braggin'," Powder Pete told Preacher. "It's bad 'nuff jist havin' to look at you." Powder Pete was so called because of his expertise with explosives.

"Did the law run him out of town?"

"Don't know. Didn't hang around to see. Law might *ask* him to leave. But if that there boy gits his back up, there ain't nobody gonna *run* him nowheres."

"Wal, les' us just sorta amble on toward the northeast," Preacher said. "If I know Smoke—and I do, I

44

raised him—he'll take his time gettin' to Bury. He'll lay back in the timber for a day 'er so and look the situation over. We'll cross the Lost River Range, head acrost the flats, and turn north, make camp in the narrows south of Bury. I know me some Flatheads live just west of the Bitterroot. Once we set up camp, I'll take me a ride over to the Divide, palaver some with 'em. They'll be our eyes and ears. That sound all right to you boys?"

"Quite inventive," Audie said.

"Ummm," Nighthawk grunted.

Buck crossed the Salmon to the east bank and began following the river north. He stayed on the fringe of the timber that made up the northern edge of the Lemhi Range. He would follow the river for about thirty-five miles before cutting to the east for about ten miles. That should put him on the outskirts of Bury. Once there, he would make camp south of the town and look it over.

The dozen mountain men, with about six hundred years of survival and fighting experience between them, were riding hard just south of Challis. With their rifles held across the saddlehorns, their fringed buckskins and animal-hide caps and brightly colored shirts and jackets and sashes, the last of the mountain men were returning for one more fight. They were riding hard to help—if he needed it—the youngest mountain man. One of their own. A young man who had chosen the lonely call of the wilderness as home. A young man who preferred the high lonesome over the towns and cities. A young man they had taken under their wing and helped to raise, imparting to him the wisdom of the wilderness, hopefully perpetuating a way of life that so-called civilized people now sneered at and rejected. This gathering, this aging motley crew knew they were the last—the very last—of a select breed of men. After this ride, never again would so many gather. But hopefully, just maybe, their young protege would live on, known for the rest of his life, as the last mountain man.

6

The town of Bury, with a population of about five hundred, sat on a road first roughed out by Mormon settlers in the mid-1850s. Bury had a bank, probably the best school in that part of the country—a large, two-story building—a large mercantile store, a weekly newspaper, several saloons, several cafes, a large hotel, a sheriff, several deputies, a jail, a leather shop, and several other businesses, including a whorehouse located discreetly outside of town. The town also boasted several churches. A handful of ranches lay around the town, and a lot of producing mines as well.

And nearly all of it was owned by three men: Stratton, Potter, and Richards.

Bury also had a volunteer fire department. They were going to need a fire department before Buck was through.

The business district of Bury was three blocks long, on both sides of the wide street. It was down that street that Buck rode at midmorning. He had camped some miles from the town, watching the one road for two days. A stagecoach rolled in every other day. Wagons bringing supplies rolled by. Peddlers and tinkers and snake-oil salesmen rattled past.

Booming little town, Buck thought. For a while longer, that is.

The first thing Buck noticed in his slow ride up the street was the number of gunhands lounging about on the boardwalk, and not just in front of the saloons. A couple always seemed to be in front of the bank, as well. Buck guessed there had been some attempts to hold up the place. Or perhaps the Big Three were just cautious men.

He located the livery stable and arranged a stall for Drifter, warning the stable boy not to enter Drifter's stall.

"He's got a mean eye for sure," the boy said, eyeballing the stallion.

"He killed one man," Buck said, knowing that tale would soon spread throughout the small town.

The boy solemnly nodded his head.

Buck handed the boy a five-dollar gold piece. "Just between you and me, now. Make certain he gets an extra ration of grain."

"Yes, *sir*!"

"Both Drifter and the packhorse, now."

"Yes, *sir*!"

Taking his personal gear and his rifle, Buck stashed the rest of his gear in Drifter's stall. He walked toward the hotel. As he walked, he passed by a very pretty, dark-haired, hazel-eyed young woman. He smiled at her and she blushed. Buck paused and watched her walk on toward the edge of town. Buck crossed the street to better watch her and saw her push open the gate on a small picket fence and walk up onto the porch of a small house. She disappeared from view.

"Nice," he muttered.

"Sure is," a voice came from behind him.

Buck slowly turned around to face the sheriff and one of his deputies. Neither one of them would win any prizes for good looks.

"Sheriff Reese. This is Rogers, one of my deputies.

I don't know you."

That's good, Buck thought. But you will, Sheriff. You will. "Buck West."

"Ahh," Reese said. "Now I know you. The gun-hand."

"Some say I am."

"Going to be in town long?"

"That depends."

"On what?"

"On how fast I get rested up, resupplied, and find out more about this Smoke Jensen and how I go about collecting the reward money."

Reese smiled. "First you have to catch him, hombre."

"I'll catch him," Buck said, without changing expression.

Reese stared at the young man. Something about this tall young man was just slightly unsettling. Even for a man like Dan Reese, who had worked on both sides of the law nearly all his life. Reese had worked the hoot-owl trails many times, in several states, ducking and dodging the law that sought him.

Beside him, Rogers stood and glared at Buck, forming an instant dislike for the young man. Rogers was big and solid, including that space between his ears. He was not just dumb; he was stupid. And very dangerous. He had killed more times than he could remember—with fists, guns, knife, or club.

"You stay away from Sally Reynolds," Rogers said. "I got my eyes on her. 'Sides, she likes me."

Buck cut his eyes to the deputy. He doubted that even Rogers's own mother liked him very much. Sally Reynolds. He wondered what the pretty lady did in Bury?

"Sally Reynolds is one of our schoolteachers," Reese said. "She wouldn't want notin' to do with no damned bounty hunter like you, West."

"Uh-huh," Buck said. "You're probably right, Sheriff. Anything else I need to know about Bury and its citizens?"

Reese got the accurate impression that he had just been dismissed by Buck. The feeling irritated him. "Jist stay out of trouble."

Buck turned his back to the men and walked on up the boardwalk, toward the hotel.

"I don't lak him," Rogers said. "I think I'll kill him."

"I don't like him either. But you don't do nothin' 'til you're told to do it. You understand that, Rogers?"

"Yes, sir."

"Let's find out what Stratton thinks about this West."

"What's your impression of him?" Stratton asked.

Reese hesitated, then leveled with one of his three bosses. He didn't much care for Buck West, but he knew better than to play the game anyway other than straight. "I think he's who he says he is. And I think the rumors are right. He's one hell of a gunfighter."

"Keep an eye on him."

"Yes, sir."

Buck checked into the hotel, a very nice one for a town so far away from the beaten path, and stowed his gear. He bathed, took a shave, and dressed in a dark suit, white shirt and black string tie, polished boots. He checked and cleaned his .44s, and belted them around his waist, tying down the low-riding holsters.

He stepped out onto the boardwalk, carefully

looked all around him, as was his habit, and then headed for the cafe, preferring that over the hotel dining room. He took a seat one table over from Miss Sally Reynolds. They were the only customers in the cafe, the lunch hour over. Buck ordered the plate lunch special and coffee. He felt eyes on him and looked up into her hazel eyes. He smiled at her.

"Pleasant day," Buck said.

"Very," Sally replied. "Now that school is out for the summer, it's especially so."

"I regret that I don't have more formal education," Buck said. "The War Between the States put a halt to that."

"It's never too late to learn, sir."

"You're a schoolteacher?"

"Yes, I am. And you? . . ."

"Drifter, ma'am."

"I . . . don't think so," the young woman said, meeting his gaze.

Buck smiled. "Oh? And why do you say that?"

"Just a guess."

"What grades do you teach?"

"Sixth, seventh, and eighth. Why do you wear two guns?"

"Habit."

"Most of the men I've seen out here have difficulty mastering one gun," Sally said. "My first day out here I saw a man shoot his big toe off trying to quick-draw. I tried very hard not to laugh, but he looked so foolish."

Buck again smiled. "I would imagine so. But I should imagine the man minus the toe failed to find the humor in it."

"I'm sure."

Conversation waned as the waitress brought their lunches. Buck just couldn't think of a way to get the

51

talk going again.

Deputy Rogers entered the cafe, sat down at the counter, and ordered coffee.

Rogers glared at Sally as she said to Buck, "Will you be in Bury long?"

"All depends, ma'am."

"Lady of your quality shouldn't oughtta be talkin' to no bounty hunter, Miz Reynolds," Rogers said. "Ain't fittin.' "

Buck slowly chewed a bite of beef.

"Mr. Rogers," Sally said. "The gentleman and I are merely exchanging pleasantries over lunch. I was addressing the gentleman, not you."

Rogers flushed, placed his coffee mug on the counter, and abruptly left the cafe.

"Deputy Rogers doesn't like me very much," Buck said.

"Why?" Sally asked bluntly.

"Because . . . I probably make him feel somewhat insecure."

"A very interesting statement from a man who professes to have little formal education, Mr.? . . ."

"West, ma'am. Buck West."

"Sally Reynolds. Western names are very quaint. Is Buck your Christian first name?"

"No, ma'am. But it might as well be. Been called that all my life."

"Are you a bounty hunter, Mr. West?"

"Bounty hunter, cowhand, gunhand, trapper. Whatever I can make a living at. You're from east of the Mississippi River, ma'am?"

"New Hampshire. I came out here last year after replying to an advertisement in a local paper. The pay is much better out here than back home."

"I . . . sort of know where New Hampshire is. I would imagine living is much more civilized back

52

there."

"To say the least, Mr. West. And also much duller."

Hang around a little longer, Sally, Buck thought. You haven't seen lively yet. "Would you walk with me, Miss Reynolds?" Buck blurted. "And please don't think I'm being too forward."

"I would love to walk with you, Mr. West."

The sun was high in the afternoon sky and Sally opened her parasol.

"Do you ride, Miss Reynolds?" Buck asked.

"Oh, yes. But I have yet to see a sidesaddle in Bury."

"They ain't too common a sight out here."

"*Ain't* is completely unacceptable in formal writing and speech, Mr. West. But I think you know that."

"Yes, ma'am. Sorry."

She tilted her head, smiling, looking at him, a twinkle in her eyes. As they walked, Buck's spurs jingled. "Which line of employment are you currently pursuing, Mr. West?"

"Beg pardon, ma'am?"

"Bounty hunter, cowhand, gunhand, or trapper?"

"I'm lookin' for a killer' named Smoke Jenson. Thirty thousand dollar reward for him."

"Quite a sum of money. I've seen the wanted posters around town. What, exactly, did this Jenson do?"

"Killed a lot of people, ma'am. He's a fast gun for hire, so I'm told."

"Faster than you, Mr. West?"

"I hope not."

She laughed at that.

A group of hard-riding cowboys took that time to burst into town, whooping and hollering and kicking up clouds of dust as they spurred their horses, sliding to a stop in front of one of the saloons.

53

Buck pulled Sally into a doorway and shielded her from the dust and flying clods.

When the dust had settled, Buck stepped aside and Sally stepped once more onto the boardwalk. "Those are men from the PSR Ranch," she said. "Rowdies and ruffians, for the most part."

"PSR?" Buck asked, knowing full well what the letters stood for.

"Potter, Stratton, Richards. It's the biggest ranch in the state, so I'm told."

"How do they get their cattle to market?" Buck asked. "I know they don't drive them over the Divide."

"They haven't made any big drives yet. I understand that so far they've sold them to people in this area. Leesburg, Salmon, Lemhi. Small communities within a fifty- to seventy-mile radius. The big drive is scheduled for late next spring. They'll be using a hundred or more cowboys."

"Quite an undertaking."

"Oh, yes."

A door opened behind them. A very pretty lady emerged from the dress shop. "Sally," she said. She gave Buck a cool glance and walked on down the boardwalk.

"That is, ah, Mr. Richards's mistress, Buck. Her name is Jane."

Buck had just seen his sister for the first time in almost ten years.

7

"You have an odd look in your eyes, Buck," Sally said.

"I never have gotten used to being snubbed, I suppose. But I suppose I should have, by now. But to be snubbed by a common whore irritates me."

"She may be a whore, but she isn't common," Sally corrected that. "I'm told she speaks three languages very fluently; her home is the showcase of the state; and her carriage was built and brought over from France."

"Oh?" Now where in the devil did Janey learn three languages? he thought. She quit school in the eighth grade.

"Here she comes now," Sally said.

It was a grand carriage, all right. The coachman was a black man, all gussied up in a military-looking outfit. Four tough-looking riders accompanied the carriage. Two to the front, two to the back.

As the carriage passed, Buck removed his hat and bowed gallantly.

Even from the boardwalk, Sally could see the woman in the carriage flush with anger and jerk her head to the front. Sally suppressed a giggle.

"Oh, you made her mad, Buck."

"She'll get over it, I reckon." Buck remembered the

time, back before the war, when he had rocked the family outhouse—with his sister in it. She'd chased him all over the farm, throwing rocks at him.

"That funny look is back in your eyes, Buck. What are you thinking?"

"My own sister," he said.

"Does Jane remind you of her?"

"Not really. I haven't seen the sister I remember in a long time. I'll probably never see that girl again."

Sally touched his arm. "Oh, Buck. Why do you say that?"

"There is nothing to return to, Sally. Everything and everyone is gone."

He took her elbow and they began to walk toward the edge of town. They had not gone half a block before the sounds of hooves drumming on the hard-packed dirt came to them. Two of the bodyguards that had been with Jane reined up in the street, turning their horses to face Buck and Sally.

Buck gently but firmly pushed Sally to one side. "Stand clear," he said in a low voice. "Trouble ahead."

"What—?" she managed to say before one of Richards's gunhands cut her off.

"You run on home now, schoolmarm. This here might git messy."

Sally stuck her chin out. "I will stand right here on this boardwalk until the soles of my shoes grow roots before I'll take orders from you, you misbegotten cretin!"

Buck grinned at her. Now this lady had some *sand* to her.

"Whut the hell did she call me?" the cowboy said to his friend.

"Durned if I know."

The cowboy swung his eyes back to Buck. "You

56

insulted Miss Janey, boy. She's madder than a tree full of hornets. You got fifteen minutes to git your gear and git gone."

"I think I'll stay," Buck said. He had thumbed the thongs off his .44s after pushing Sally to one side.

"Boy," the older and uglier of the bodyguards said, "do you know who I am?"

"Can't say I've had the pleasure," Buck replied.

"Name's Dickerson, from over Colorado way. That ring a bell in your head?"

It did, but Buck didn't let it show. Dickerson was a top gun. No doubt about that. Not only was he mean, he was cat quick with a pistol. "Nope. Sorry."

"And this here," Dickerson jerked a thumb, "is Russell."

Buck hadn't heard of Russell, but he figured if the guy rode with Dickerson, he'd be good. "Pleased to meet you," Buck said politely.

Dickerson gave Buck an exasperated look. "Boy, are you stupid or tryin' to be smart-mouthed?"

"Neither one. Now if you gentlemen will excuse me, I'd like to continue my stroll with Miss Reynolds."

Both Dickerson and Russell dismounted, ground-reining their ponies. "Only place you goin' is carried to Boot Hill, boy."

Several citizens had gathered around to watch the fun, including one young cowhand with a weather-beaten face and a twinkle in his eyes.

"Stand clear," Buck told the crowd.

The gathering crowd backed up and out of the line of impending fire. They hoped.

"I've bothered no one," Buck said to the crowd, without taking his eyes from the two gunhands facing him. "And I'm not looking for a fight. But if I'm pushed, I'll fight. I just wanted that made public."

"Git on your hoss and ride, boy!" Russell said. "And do it right now."

"I'm staying."

"You a damn fool, boy!" Dickerson said. "But if you want a lead supper, that's up to you."

"Lead might fly in both directions," Buck said calmly. "Were I you, I'd think about that."

Some odd light flickered quickly through Dickerson's eyes. He wasn't used to being sassed or disobeyed. But damn this boy's eyes, he didn't seem to be worried at all. Who in the devil was they up against?

"That's Buck West, Dickerson," the young cowboy with the beat-up face said.

"That don't spell road apples to me," Russell said. He glared at Buck. "Move, tinhorn, or the undertaker's gonna be divvyin' up your pocket money."

"I like it here," Buck said.

"Then draw, damn you!" Dickerson shouted. He went for his gun. Out of the corner of his eye, he saw Russell grab for his .45.

Buck's hands swept down and up with the speed of an angry striking snake. His matched .44s roared and belched smoke and flame. The ground-reined horses snorted and reared at the noise. Dickerson and Russell lay on the dusty street. Both were badly wounded. The guns of the PSR men lay beside them in the dirt. Neither had had time to cock and fire.

"Jumpin' jackrabbits!" the young cowboy said. "I never seen nothin' like that in my life."

Buck calmly punched out the spent brass and dropped the empties to the dirt. He reloaded and holstered his .44s, leaving the hammer thongs off.

Sheriff Dan Reese and Deputy Rogers came at a run up the wide street. Many townspeople had gathered on the boardwalks to crane their necks.

"Drop those damn guns, West!" Reese yelled before arriving at the scene. "You're under arrest."

"I'd like to know why." Sally said, stepping up to stand beside Buck. Her face was very pale. She pointed to Dickerson and Russell. "Those hooligans started it. They ordered Mr. West to leave town. When he refused, they threatened to kill him. They drew first. And I'll swear to that in a court of law."

"She's right, Sheriff," the young cowhand said.

Reese gave the cowboy an ugly look. "Which side are you on, Sam?"

"The side of right, Sheriff."

Dickerson cried out in pain. The front of his shirt was covered with blood. The .44 slug had hit him squarely in the chest, ricocheted off the breast bone, and exited out the top of his shoulder, tearing a great jagged hole as it spun away.

Russell was the hardest hit. Buck's .44 had struck him in the stomach and torn out his lower back. The gunhand was not long for this world and everybody looking at him knew it.

"Any charges, Sheriff?" Buck asked, his voice steady and low.

There was open dislike in Reese's eyes as he glared at Buck. He stepped closer. "You're trouble, West. And you and me both know it. I hope you crowd me, gunfighter. 'Cause when you do, I'll kill you!"

"You'll try," Buck replied in the same low tone.

Reese flushed. He stepped back. "No charges, West. It was a fair fight."

Russell groaned, blood leaking from his mouth. He jerked once on the dirt and died.

"Have his full name recorded," Buck said, playing the part of the hard hunter. "There might be a reward on him."

"You're a sorry son of a you-know-what," Reese said. "Ain't you got no feelins at all?"

"Only for those who deserve it," Buck said. He turned and took Sally's elbow. "Shall we continue?"

As the tall young gunfighter and the pretty lady strolled off, the young cowpuncher named Sam looked at them. He thought he knew who the gunfighter was, and his name wasn't Buck West. But Sam thought he'd keep that information to himself for a time. Might come in handy.

"Your first gunfight?" Buck asked as they walked.

"Yes. And I hope my last."

"It won't be. Not if you continue living out here. It's a big, wild, raw country still. The laws are simple and straight to the point. Justice comes down hard. Out here, a man's word is his bond. That's the way it should be everywhere. Tinhorns and shysters and crooks don't last long in the west."

"And you, Buck?"

"What do you mean?"

"Will you last long out here?"

"No way I can answer that. I hung up my guns once. Thought I would never put them on again. It didn't work out. Maybe I can walk away from it one more time. I don't know. Worth a try, I guess."

They paused at Sally's front gate. "Would you like to have supper with me this evening?" Buck asked. "At the hotel dining room?"

"You're awfully young to have already retired once from gunfighting."

"Some of us had to start young, Sally."

"Yes. I suppose. It's an interesting land, your wild west. I'll be ready at six. Good afternoon, Mr. Buck West." She smiled. "Or whatever your name is."

Jane looked out the window of her bedroom. Ever since she had seen the arrogant young man she had struggled to recall where she'd seen him before. She knew she had. But where? She just could not remember. And now the startling news that the young man had bested Russell and Dickerson in a stand-up gunfight.

Incredible.

She sighed and turned away from the window that overlooked the northern vastness of the PSR ranchlands. She had time for a bath before Stratton and Richards and wives came out for their monthly business and dinner meeting.

The face of the tall gunslick remained in her mind. His name would come to her in time.

Sheriff Dan Reese had gone through all his dodgers twice, looking for anyone who resembled Buck West. Nothing. But anybody that fast and sure had to have a backtrail. Trick was in finding it. Russell and Dickerson were both hard men. Or had been. And they both had been almighty quick. Yet this Buck West had handled them as easily as children. Just blew in out of nowhere. Probably came from Texas, 'way down on the border.

Sheriff Reese stood up and stretched. One thing for certain, he thought: Buck West was trouble. Best way to handle him was to get him on the PSR payroll. He'd talk to Richards about it. First thing this evening.

He glanced up at the clock. Had to shave and bath now, though. Get out to PSR headquarters.

The dozen old mountain men made their camp about ten miles south of the town of Bury, in the timber of the Lemhi Range. As soon as they were set up, Preacher changed ponies and headed east, toward the Continental Divide and the Bitterroot Range. At first light, Dupre was to head into Bury for a look-see. Pick up some bacon and beans and coffee and salt and keep his ear open.

"Better wash them jug-handle things first," Beartooth told him. "Probably git five pounds of dirt out of 'um."

"I'd talk," Dupre retorted. "Last time you took a bath it killed the fish for five miles downstream."

"Ummm," Nighthawk said.

8

Buck had ordered his one suit pressed, had bought a new set of longhandles and a new pearl-gray shirt, and was ready to knock on Miss Sally Reynolds's door promptly at six.

As he walked the short blocks from the hotel to Sally's house, Buck had been conscious of eyes on him. Not unfriendly eyes, but curious ones. He had passed several ladies during his walk. They had batted their eyes and swished their bustles at him. Buck had smiled at the ladies and continued walking, his spurs jingling.

He had spoken to the crowd of little boys that had followed him—at a safe distance. He had noticed that several of them were wearing two wooden guns in makeshift holsters, the leather tied down low.

Buck didn't know whether he liked that or not. He didn't want any young people aping his lifestyle. But he didn't know what he could do about it.

Miss Sally Reynolds was dressed in gingham; a bright summer color with matching parasol. The light, bright color setting off her dark hair. She wore just a touch of rouge on her cheeks.

Dusk when they closed the gate to her picket fence and began their stroll to the hotel dining room. The crowd of boys had been called in to supper by their mothers, so Buck and Sally could walk in peace.

They had just left Sally's house when two carriages,

accompanied by half a dozen outriders, rolled stately past them.

"Wiley and Linda Potter in the first carriage," Sally said. "Keith and Lucille Stratton in the second carriage. They're going out to Josh Richards's. He lives on the PSR Ranch. They have a monthly dinner and business meeting. The sheriff will be there too, I should imagine."

"Same time, every month?" Buck asked.

"Oh, yes. Very punctual and predictable."

Buck smiled at that. But his smile was only to hide his true inner feelings. And those thoughts were dark and dangerous.

For one hot, flashing instant, Buck's thoughts were flung back in time.

La Plaza de los Leones—Square of the Lions, later to be renamed Walsenburg—was a major farming and ranching community in 1869, when Smoke and Preacher rode in from the west.

They were met by the town marshal and told to keep on riding.

They planned to do just that. But first they wanted to know about the Casey ranch.

"Southeast of here. On the flats. Casey's got eight hands. They all look like gunnies."

"You got an undertaker in this town?" Smoke asked.

"Sure. Why?"

"Tell him to dust off his boxes—he's about to get some business."

Ten miles out of town, they met two hands riding easy, heading into town.

"You boys is on TC range," one of the riders warned. "Get the hell off. The boss don't like strangers and neither do I."

Smoke smiled. "You boys been ridin' for the brand

long?"

"You deef?" the second hand asked. "You been told to git—now git!"

"You answer my question and then maybe we'll leave."

"Since '66. That's when we pushed them longhorns up here from Texas. If that's any of your damned business. Now git!"

"Who owns TC?"

"Ted Casey. Boy, are you plumb crazy or jist stupid?"

"My Pa knew a Ted Casey. Fought in the war with him—for the Gray."

"Oh? What be your name?"

"Some people call me Smoke." He grinned. "Jensen."

Recognition flared in the eyes of the TC riders. They grabbed for their guns. They were far too slow. Smoke's left-hand .36 belched flame and smoke as Preacher fired his Henry one-handed. Horses reared and snorted and bucked at the noise. The TC gunnies dropped from their saddles, dead and dying.

The one TC gunhand alive pulled himself up on one elbow. Blood poured from two chest wounds, the blood pink and frothy, one .36 ball having passed through both lungs, taking the rider as he turned in the saddle.

"Heard you was comin'," he gasped. "You quick, no doubt 'bout that. Your brother was easy." He smiled a bloody smile. "Potter shot him low in the back; took him a long time to die. Died hard. Hollered a lot." The TC rider closed his eyes and died.

Smoke and Preacher burned the house down, driving the men from it after a prolonged gunfight. They took only Casey alive.

"What you figurin' on doin' with him?" Preacher

65

asked.

"I figure on going back to town and hanging him."

"I don't know how you got that mean streak, boy. Seein' as how you was raised—partly—by a gentle old man like me."

Despite the death he had brought and the destruction wrought, Smoke had to laugh at that. Preacher was known throughout the West as one of the most dangerous men ever to roam the high country and vast Plains. The old mountain man had once gone on the prowl, spending two years of his life tracking down and killing—one by one—a group of men who ambushed and killed a friend of his, stealing the man's furs.

Smoke tied the unconscious Casey across a saddle. " 'Course you never went on the hunt for anyone, right?"

"Well . . . mayhaps once or twice. But that was years back. I've mellowed a mite since then."

"Sure." Smoke grinned. Preacher was still as mean as a cornered puma.

By the banks of a creek outside of town, a crowd had gathered for the hanging. Marshal Crowell was furious as he watched Smoke build a noose.

"This man has not been tried!" the marshal protested.

"Yeah, he has," Smoke said. "He admitted to me what he done."

The marshal looked at the smoke to the southeast.

"House fire," Preacher said. "Poor feller lost everything."

Casey spat in the direction of the crowd. He cursed them.

"This is murder!" the marshal said. "I intend to file charges against you both."

"Halp!" Casey hollered.

A local minister began praying for Casey's poor wretched soul.

Casey soiled himself as the noose was slipped around his neck.

The minister prayed harder.

"That ain't much of a prayer," Preacher opined sourly. "I had you beat hands down when them Injuns was fixin' to skin me alive on the Platte. Put some feelin' in it, man!"

The local minister began to shout and sweat. The crowd swelled; some had brought their supper with them. A hanging was always an interesting sight. There just wasn't that much to do in small western towns. Some men were betting how long it would take for Casey to die—providing his neck didn't snap when his butt left the saddle.

A small choir had assembled. The ladies lifted their voices to the sky.

Shall We Gather At The River, they intoned.

"I personally think Swing Low would be more like it," Preacher opined.

A local merchant looked at Casey. "You owe me sixty-five dollars."

"Hell with you!" Casey tried to kick the man.

"I want my money!" the merchant shouted.

"You got anything to say before you go to Hell?" Smoke asked Casey.

"You won't get away with this!" Casey screamed. "If Potter or Stratton don't git you, Richards will."

"What's he talkin' about?" the marshal asked.

"Casey was with the Gray—same as my Pa and brother," Smoke explained. "Casey and some others waylaid a patrol bringing a load of gold into Georgia. They shot my brother in the back and left him to die. Hard."

"That was war," the marshal said.

67

"It was murder."

"Hurry up," a citizen shouted. "My supper's gettin' cold."

"I'll see you hang for this," the marshal told Smoke.

"You go to hell!" Smoke told him.

Casey swung in the cool, late afternoon air.

"I'm notifying the territorial governor of this," the marshal said.

Casey's bootheels drummed the air.

"Shout, man!" Preacher told the minister. "Sing, sisters, sing!" he urged the choir.

"What about my sixty-five dollars?" the merchant shouted.

All the memories had flashed through Buck's mind in the space of two heartbeats.

"You've gone away again," Sally said.

Buck looked at her. She was smiling up at him. "Yes, I guess I was, Sally. I apologize for that."

They continued walking toward the hotel. Sally said, "Buck are you here to slay dragons or to tilt at windmills?"

"Beg pardon?"

"Are you familiar with Cervantes?"

"Is he a gunhand?"

She looked at him to see if he was serious. He was. "No, Buck. A writer."

"No, I guess I missed that one. I know what slaying dragons means. But what's that about tilting windmills?"

"Oh, I suppose you're not. I didn't notice Sancho riding in with you."

Now Buck was thoroughly confused. "I never had a Mex sidekick, Sally."

"I have a copy of Don Quixote—somewhere. I'll find it and loan it to you. I think you'll enjoy it."

"All right." Buck was well-read, considering his lack of formal education and allowing for the locale and his lifestyle. But he sure as hell had never heard of any Don Quixote.

Heads turned as they entered the dining room. Some dining there gave the young couple disapproving looks. A few smiled. They took a table next to the wall, affording them maximum privacy, and ordered supper. PSR beef, naturally, with boiled potatoes and beans, and apple pie for dessert.

Neither admitted it, for separate reasons, but both wondered what might be taking place at the grand house of the PSR ranch.

"And it was a fair fight?" Josh Richards asked Sheriff Reese.

"Stand up and square," Reese said. "I didn't see it, but Sam did. He said he ain't never seen nothin' like that Buck West's draw. Lightnin' fast. Neither Dickerson nor Russell got a shot off. And they drew first."

"And he's a bounty hunter?" Stratton asked. He was a big man gone to fat. Diamond rings glittered on his soft fat fingers.

"That's what Jerry told me."

"Jerry saw him fight back at the trading post, that right?" Potter asked.

"Yes, sir."

Wiley Potter, like his two partners, had pushed his past from him. He almost never thought of his outlaw and traitor days. He was a successful man, a man under consideration to be territorial governor. And he played his political power to the hilt. He was always well dressed, well groomed.

Josh Richards listened, but had little to say on the subject of the bounty hunter, Buck West. If this West was as good as described, Richards wanted him on the payroll. Of the three men, Richards had changed the least. Physically. He was still a powerful man. Something he had always been proud of. That and his reputation with the ladies. But he knew it was time for him to be thinking of settling down. And while Janey's reputation was a bit scarlet, she was, nevertheless, the woman he planned to marry. She was just as ruthless and cunning as Richards. Would do anything for money. They made a good team.

"I'll see him in the morning," Richards said. "Let's eat. I'm hungry."

Potter was big politically—the front man, all smiles and congeniality, territory-wide. Stratton was the local big shot—the president of the bank and so forth. But Richards ran the show, always staying quietly in the background. That's the way he wanted it.

The men trouped out of the study into the dining room. Richards looked at Jane. "Something the matter?" he asked in a whisper.

"That Buck West. I've seen him before. Somewhere."

"Can you remember where?"

She shook her head. "Not yet. But I will." She looked him directly in the eyes. "He's trouble, Josh."

"Your imagination, my dear. He'd be a good man to have on our side."

"Watch him," she cautioned. "I don't trust him."

"You don't even *know* him, Jane!"

"Yeah, I do. I just can't remember where I met him, that's all."

"It'll come to you."

"Bet on it."

70

9

Buck knew he wasn't going to tolerate much living in the hotel. He didn't like the closed-in feeling. The sheets were clean, and that was nice, but the bed was soft and made his back hurt. Buck was not accustomed to the finer things in life. So-called finer things. To Buck, the finer things were the clean smell of deep timber; the high thinness of clean air in the mountains; the rush of a surging stream, wild white water whipping and singing; the cough of a puma and the calling of a bird. Now *that* was fine living!

He walked down to the cafe in the coolness of the early morning. The eastern sky was just beginning to streak with silver, but the cafe was busy, the smell of bacon and eggs and frying potatoes filling the air.

Conversation stopped when Buck walked in and took a seat at a far table, his back to the wall. When the waitress came to take his order, Buck said, "If the food's as good as it smells, I'll take one of everything on the menu."

The waitress smiled at him. Buck ordered breakfast and said, "The owner must make a fortune in this place, the food's so good."

"The owner?" the waitress asked, a curious look in her eyes.

"Yes. Are you the owner?"

She laughed. "Not hardly, sir. Mr. Stratton is the owner. Mr. Stratton owns everything in Bury. Every building and every business."

"Interesting," Buck said. "*Everything?*"

"Everything, sir."

Buck mulled that over in his mind while he ate. The buzz of conversation had returned to normal and the townspeople were ignoring Buck, concentrating on eating. Eating was serious business in the west. Not to be taken lightly. Not at all. Buck thought, the waitress might think Stratton owns everything in sight, but Potter and Richards are right in there as well.

So no one owns their own business. Good. That will make it easier when I burn the damn place to the ground.

Buck was halfway through his breakfast when Deputy Rogers blundered in, closing the door just a bit too hard. Obviously, he wanted everyone to know he had arrived.

Rogers plopped down in a chair facing Buck and said, "Mr. Richards wants to see you."

"When I finish eating. Now go away."

Rogers could not believe his ears. "Hey, gunslick! I said—"

"I heard what you said. So did the entire crowd. I'll see Mr. Richards when I'm finished. Now go away."

Rogers wanted to start something. He wanted it so badly he could taste his personal rage. But he had orders to leave Buck alone. Uttering an oath, he stumbled from the table and slammed the door behind him.

The cafe was totally silent. Even the cook had stepped out and was staring in disbelief at Buck. The one collective thought among them all was, *No one, absolutely* no one *keeps Mr. Richards waiting.*

The front door opened. Josh Richards stepped in. He nodded politely to the crowd and walked to Buck's table, pulling out a chair and calling to the waitress to bring him coffee.

"Ham and eggs are real fine," Buck said. "I recommend them."

Richards smiled. "All right. Ham and eggs, Ruby!"

"Yes, sir."

Buck held out his right hand. "Buck West."

Richards took the offered hand. "Josh Richards. You don't much care for Deputy Rogers, do you, Mr. West?"

"I don't think he's got both hands in the stirrups, that's for sure."

"Quaint way of putting it. I'll have to remember that. Oh, you're right, Mr. West. Rogers is a bit weak between the ears. But he does what he is told to do."

"That's important to you, Mr. Richards?"

"Very."

"Money's right, I can be as loyal as any man. More than most, I reckon."

"I imagine you can. Are you looking for a job, Mr. West?"

"I'm lookin' for Smoke Jensen, sir. But that gunhand's backtrail is some cold."

"Yes. I've had a lot of men looking for Jensen. So far, to no avail. Tell you what I'll do, Mr. West. I can put you on the payroll today. Right now. Fighting wages. That's good money. Five or six times what the average puncher makes. You hang around town, the ranch. Just let your presence be known. Every now and then, I'll have a job for you. Sometimes, Mr. Stratton, Mr. Potter, or myself have to transfer large sums of money from place to place. Highwaymen have taken several of those pouches. I need a good man to

73

see that it doesn't happen again. How about it?"

"All right," Buck said with a smile. "Oh, one more thing?"

"Certainly."

Buck pointed with his fork. "Eat your breakfast. It's getting cold."

Buck met Stratton and Potter. It was all he could do to conceal his raw hatred from the men. He shook hands with them and smiled, nodding in all the right places.

When the meeting was over, he returned to his hotel room and washed his hands with lye soap. They still felt dirty to him.

He saw to his horses and found the livery boy true to his word. Both Drifter and the pack animal were getting extra rations of grain.

He walked the town, getting to know the layout of Bury. As he walked, he noticed a buckskin-clad old mountain man leaning against the wall of the not-yet-opened general store. The mountain man appeared not to be watching Buck, but Buck knew he was watching him. His name came to Buck. Dupre. The Louisiana Frenchman. He remembered him from the rendezvous at the ruins of Bent's Ford, back in . . . was it '66? Buck thought it had been.

Dupre looked as old as time itself, and as solid as a granite mountain. Buck had been raised among mountain men, and he knew these old boys were still dangerous as grizzly bears. Not a one of the mountain men still left alive could tell you how many men they'd killed. White men. Indians didn't count.

When Buck again caught his eyes, Dupre was talking to the store owner. Not owner, Buck corrected himself—manager. The two men went inside. Buck continued walking. Unlike most men who spent their lives on the hurricane deck of a horse, Buck enjoyed a good stroll.

It was a pretty little town, Buck thought. And not just thrown haphazardly together, like so many frontier towns. He took his time, speaking to the men and doffing his hat to the ladies he passed. He noticed suspicion in many of the eyes; open hostility in a like amount. He wondered about that.

"You're up early," a voice called from Buck's left.

He stopped and slowly turned. Sally Reynolds sat on her front porch, drinking what Buck guessed was coffee.

"I enjoy the early morning, Sally."

"So do I. Would you care for a cup of tea?"

"Tea?"

"Tea."

"Sure. I guess so. Never acquired much of a taste for it."

"I can make coffee."

"No, no. Tea will be fine. He pushed open the gate and took a chair on the porch.

It wasn't fine. Buck thought he was going to gag on the stuff. It didn't taste like nothing. But he smiled bravely and swallowed. Hard.

Sally laughed at him. "Please let me make you some coffee, Buck. It will only take a few minutes."

"Maybe you'd better. I sure would appreciate it. This stuff and me just don't get along."

Buck sat alone on the small porch and watched as Dupre rode past, riding slowly, his Henry repeating rifle held in one hand, across the saddle. As he rode past, the old mountain man nodded his head to Buck. "Nice mornin', ain't it, son?"

"Yes, it is. Have yourself a good day."

"My good days are twenty year down my backtrail," Dupre said. "But I still manage to git by." He rode on, soon out of sight.

"Who in the *world* was that?" Sally asked. She placed a cup of coffee on the small table between their chairs.

"You probably read about them in school," Buck said. "Mountain men?"

"Oh, yes! But I thought they were all dead."

"Most of them are. The real mountain men, that is. But there's still some salty ol' boys out there, still riding the high lonesome."

"The high lonesome? That's beautiful, Buck. Do I detect a wistful note in your voice?"

"Wistful?"

"Means a longing, or a yearning for something."

Could he trust her? Buck didn't know. She could very well be a spy for Stratton or Potter or Richards. Then he remembered how she had stood up to Sheriff Reese. He made up his mind. All right, he would tell her just enough to bait her.

"I guess so, Sally. I came out here just a boy. Alone," he lied. "I grew up in the mountains. Met a lot of mountain men. They was, were, old men even then. But tough and hard as nails. They knew their way of life was about gone, even then. But it was a fine way of life—for them; not for everybody."

"And for you, Buck?"

"For me? Do you mean did I enjoy it?"

She nodded.

Buck smiled. "Oh, yes. I'll get a burr under my saddle one of these days and you won't see me for several days. I'll have to shake the staleness of town off me; head for the high country. Me and the horses. But I'll be back. If it matters to you, that is."

She was silent for a very long moment. So long that Buck thought he had offended her with the statement.

76

"Yes, Buck. I think it does matter to me. In . . . a way that I can't explain. Not just yet. Buck, I am a very perceptive person . . ."

"A what kind of person?"

"Perceptive. That means I have a keen insight, or understanding, of things."

"Terrible to be as ignorant as I am," Buck said.

Sally did not pursue that, for she did not believe Buck to be an ignorant person. Just a person who was hiding something. For whatever reason.

"And your insight tells you what about me, Sally?"

"That you don't fully trust me."

"I don't fully trust anybody, Sally. Out here in the west, trust is something that has to be earned. It has to be that way 'cause your life might depend on it."

"Yes. I've heard that from several people since I've been out here."

"It's very true. You have a lot of outlaws working out here. You have a half-dozen Indian tribes on the warpath. Long as you stay close to Bury, you probably won't have to worry about the Indians attacking. It's too big for them. But get a mile away from town, and your life is in constant danger. You've got to know the man or men you ride with. Will they stand with you or turn tail and run? See what I mean about earning trust?"

"Yes. I suppose so. I won't tell you what else my insight tells me about you, Buck. Not until I've earned your trust. Do you suppose that will happen?"

"I imagine so."

Buck checked in with the Big Three's office manager, the office located in a building in the center of town, and told the dour-faced and sour-dispositioned little man he was riding out; be gone for a day or two.

77

Give his horse some exercise.

MacGregor grunted and told Buck to be back day after tomorrow. He had to ride south to deliver a pouch.

"I'll be back."

He rode north out of Bury, following the Salmon River. He headed for a small town called Salmon. A rough-and-tumble mining camp.

He had no intention of going to Salmon; Buck just wanted to see if he was being followed. He wanted to test how much trust Richards had in him.

"Not much," Buck grunted. He was back in the deep timber, hidden, watching his backtrail. He was watching a half-dozen riders slowly tracking him. Using his spyglass, Buck pulled them into closer view. He knew their faces, having seen them loafing around Bury, but didn't know their names.

Buck rode deeper into the timber, making a slow circle, coming out of the timber behind the riders. Now he was tracking them. He wore an amused look on his face as he watched the gunhands slowly circling, having lost Buck's trail, trying to once more find it. Buck rode up to within five hundred or so yards of the men and sat his horse, watching the men.

One rider finally lifted his head, feeling, sensing eyes on him. "Crap!" the man's voice drifted faintly to Buck. "He's watchin' *us*, boys."

The PSR riders bunched and rode slowly toward Buck, reining up a respectable distance from him. One said, "This ain't nothin' personal, partner. We ride for the brand, just like you."

"No offense taken, boys. Town was closing in on me. I wanted some space. You know what I mean?"

"Know exactly what you mean," a scar-faced rider said. "We got biscuits and coffee and it's 'bout noon. Let's build a fire and jaw some."

Cinches loosened, bits out, the horses ground-reined, they grazed. The riders sat on the ground, munching biscuits and drinking cups of strong black coffee. The scar-faced rider was Joiner. The oldest of the man, a hard-eyed puncher, was Wilson. Buck took an immediate dislike for Wilson and he sensed the feeling was mutual. McNeil had practically nothing to say. But he kept eyeballing Buck. The man's head was totally bald. Long was short and stocky. He wore one gun tied down low and his second gun in a shoulder-holster rig. Davis was a long lean drink of water; looked like a strong wind would blow him slap out of the saddle. Simpson was big and mean-looking.

"You familiar with Brown's Hole?" Joiner asked Buck.

"Been there. Went there lookin' for Jensen. Grave close to the base of Zenobia Peak. Looks like that's where Jensen planted his pa."

"You dig the grave up?" Wilson asked.

"*Hell*, no!"

Davis said, "That'd be a sin. Sorry no good would do that. Let a man rest in peace."

Wilson looked pained. "Mayhaps that'd be where the gold is buried."

"How would a dead man do that?" Simpson asked.

Wilson nodded his head. "Ain't thought about that. You right."

Then another puzzle of the mystery plopped into place in Buck's mind.

10

1867. Emmett Jensen's horses had been picketed close to the base of Zenobia Peak. His gear was by his grave, covered with a ground sheet and secured with rocks. The letter from his pa, given him by the old mountain man, Grizzly, was in Smoke's pocket.

"You read them words on that paper your pa left you?" Preacher asked.

"Not yet."

"I'll go set up camp at the Hole. I reckon you'll be along directly."

"Tomorrow. 'Bout noon."

"See you then." Preacher headed north. He would cross Vermillion Creek, then cut west into the Hole. Smoke would find him when he felt ready for human company. But for now, the young man needed to be alone with his pa.

Smoke unsaddled his horse, Seven, and allowed him to roll. He stripped the gear from the pack animals, setting them grazing. Taking a small hammer and a miner's spike from his gear, Smoke began the job of chiseling his father's name into a large, flat rock. He could not remember exactly when his pa was born, but he thought it about 1815.

Headstone in place, secured by rocks, Smoke built a small fire, put coffee on to boil in the blackened pot, then sat down to read the letter from his pa.

Son,

I found some of the men who killed your brother Luke and stolt the gold that belonged to the Gray. Theys more of them than I first thought. I killed two of the men work for them, but they got led in me and I had to hitail it out. Came here. Not goin to make it. Son, you dont owe nuttin to the Cause of the Gray. So dont get in in your mind you do. Make yoursalf a good life and look to my final restin place if you need help.

Preacher kin tell you some of what happen, but not all. Remember—look to my grave if you need help.

I allso got word that your sis Janey leff that gambler and has took up with an outlaw down in Airyzona. Place called Tooson. I woodn fret much about her. She is mine, but I think she is trash. Dont know where she got that streek from.

I am gettin tared and seein is hard. Lite fadin. I love you Kirby-Smoke.

Pa

Smoke reread the letter. Look to my grave. He could not understand that part. He pulled up his knees and put his head on them, feeling he ought to cry, or something. But no tears came.

Now he was alone. He had no other kin, and he did not count his sister as kin. He had his guns, his horses, a bit of gold, and his friend, Preacher.

He was eighteen years old.

Now, five years later, it all came back to him. Sure,

he thought. His pa had dug his own grave, put the gold in the bottom, and then crawled in on top of it to die. The old mountain man, Grizzly, had buried him.

Well, the gold could just stay there. Damned if he'd dig up his pa's grave for it.

"Where else you been lookin' for this Smoke?" McNeil asked.

"Name someplace. I thought I had him cornered over near Pagosa Springs, but he gave me the slip. I drifted down into New Mexico Territory after him. But he was always one jump ahead of me. He's slick."

"He'll screw up," Long said.

"When he does I'm gonna be there," Buck said. And he noticed out of the corner of his eyes that the men seemed to relax. He had passed their test.

Buck prowled the area about Bury for two days, planting a permanent map in his brain. He would remember the trails and roads and landmarks. They would come in handy when Buck made his move and sought his escape.

And he learned from the PSR gunhands about the townspeople of Bury. They were a pretty scummy lot, according to the riders. There were men who had skipped out on partners back east; men who were wanted for everything from petty crimes to murder. In exchange for loyalty, the Big Three had offered them sanctuary and a chance to bury their past. After twenty years, the businesses they ran for the Big Three would revert to the shopkeepers. Free and clear.

So Buck could expect no help from them.

In a way, that knowledge made it easier.

The saddlebags handed to Buck by MacGregor

were heavy. The canvas and leather saddlebags were flap-secured by padlocks. Buck did not ask what was in the bags; the sour little Scotsman did not volunteer that information.

"It's about a sixty-five-mile ride," Buck was told. "Head out east to the Lemhi River and follow it down. Little mining operation down in the Lemhi Valley. Town ain't got no name. So it's called No Name. Be a man there waitin' for you. Name is Rex. Give the saddlebags to him, wait 'til he checks them out, and he'll give you a receipt. Come back here."

The Scotsman turned away and stumped back to his rolltop desk, leaving Buck with the heavy bags. Buck smiled. "Gimme some expense money, friend."

The Scotsman sighed and reached into a tin box, pulling out a thin sheaf of bills. He made Buck sign for them. "Bring back anything that's left. Not that I think there will be anything left, that is."

Buck rode out at nine that morning. He stopped by Sally's place and found her sitting on the front porch. Drinking that damnable tea. "Be back in about three days." He smiled. "I'll bring you back a couple of pounds of coffee." He wheeled Drifter and was gone.

Staying close to the timber, with the flats to his left, Buck let Drifter pick his own pace. About ten miles out of town he reined up and sat his horse. He rubbed his eyes in disbelief. Was that an elf up ahead, sitting on a spotted pony? Buck walked Drifter slowly toward the sight. Sure looked like an elf.

"Since I care nothing for life in caves or other subterranean dwellings, I can assure you that I am not a troll," the little man said, when Buck was within earshot.

"A what?"

"Never mind, young man. My name is Audie. I, along with others of our vanishing breed, have made

83

our meager camp just to the west of where we are now engaged in this somewhat less than loquacious confabulation."

Buck blinked. "Huh?"

Audie sighed. "Very well." He took a deep breath. "Me and them there other ol' boys who was pards with Preacher is a-camped over yonder." He jerked his thumb.

"Oh. All right. For a little fellow you got a smart mouth, you know that?"

Audie jerked out a .44 with the barrel sawed off short. "But I carry a very large friend, do I not?"

"I'd say so. An' quick with it, too."

"Did you think I might be an elf?" Audie smiled after the question.

"Well, sir. Ah . . . yeah!"

"How quaint," the remark was very drily given. "But . . . given the fact that elves are rumored to engage in somewhat capricious interference in human affairs, and are usually represented in diminutive human form, I suppose your first impression might be forgiven. But I cannot, for the life of me, envision Graybull as an elf."

"Mister Audie, I don't *even* know what it is you just said."

"We're watching you," Audie plunged onward, undaunted. "We'll be there when you need us." He wheeled his pony around and trotted off.

Buck watched him disappear from view. Buck removed his hat and scratched his head. "I've seen the seasons change, the birthing of human life, and been in love. But I ain't *never* seen nothin' like that!"

At No Name, Buck tied up in front of a building with the name PSR on the false front. *Rex Augsman* was painted on the door. Buck pushed open the door and stepped inside, pausing for a moment to allow his eyes to adjust to the dimmer light.

"You Rex Augsman?" Buck asked the man who was rising from behind his desk.

"That's me."

"You got some proof of that?"

He pointed to a diploma hanging on the wall. Mining engineer. Rex M. Augsman.

"I'm from PSR headquarters up in Bury." He held out the saddlebags. "I'm supposed to give this to you."

"You look like you might just have some sense," Rex said. "A definite improvement over the others." He opened the padlocks and looked inside. He smiled and said, "Welcome to the team. You passed the final test."

"What do you mean?" Buck asked.

The engineer dumped the contents of the heavy saddlebags onto the counter. The bags had been filled with cut-up pieces of newspaper and lots of rocks.

"The young man is not exactly a paragon of intelligence," Audie said. "But there is something about him that suggests there might be a glimmer of hope."

"Smart as a whip, you dwarf!" Preacher fired at the former schoolteacher. Halfway to the Divide, Preacher had run into a band of friendly Flatheads. Yes, they had been into Bury many times to trade. Yes, they would keep their eyes and ears open and report back to Preacher. Preacher had returned to the base camp.

"No doubt you speak nonprejudicially," Audie said.

"Don't you cuss me!" Preacher warned. "I'll rap you up-side the head."

Audie reached for the sawed-off .44. Preacher reached for his Colt.

Lobo suddenly growled like a wolf and the two old friends settled down, dropping their hands from the butts of pistols.

"Sorry 'bout that, little friend," Preacher said.

"I, too, offer my sincere apologies, Preacher," Audie said. "It's the tension of waiting for the unknown."

Dupre grinned and walked to his bedroll. He pulled two clay jugs out of the blankets. "I tink perhaps we hav a drink or three," he said.

"Right good idee," Greybull said.

"I could stand a taste myself," Matt said. "How 'bout you, Nighthawk?"

"Ummm."

Buck had asked for a receipt for the newspapers and rocks. Back in Bury, he solemnly presented it to MacGregor. The Scotsman looked at Buck, then the receipt, and a sour smile slowly formed on his lips.

"You're a damn fool for staying, boy," MacGregor said. "I told Richards you were an honest man. That impressed him. But honest men won't last long in a town filled with scallawags and hooligans. Tell him I said it, if you wish—but you won't. You've stepped into a snake pit, young man. There isn't a handful of people—men *and* women—in this town and surrounding area that is worth spit. Oh, I know why you're here, Mr. Kirby Jensen, aka Smoke, aka Buck West. You're here to avenge your wife, your son, your father, your friend Preacher. You're so full of hate it's consuming you, eating you alive. If you let it, boy, it will destroy you."

"How many others know who I am?" Buck asked, keeping his voice calm.

"I think the red-haired gunman, Sam, probably

knows. Sam is quite like you. An honest man. The schoolteacher you've been sparking about, Sally. She probably suspects. Don't worry about me, Buck. I am a federal marshal."

11

Buck had asked the Scotsman how he had known about him. MacGregor had shown him a wanted dodger on Smoke. He had cut off the hair and added a beard. It was eerie; almost like looking into a mirror.

"Your skill and speed with your guns gave you away, Buck," MacGregor said. Then he smiled. "What are you planning to do here?"

"I'm going to kill Potter and Richards and Stratton and then burn this damn town to the ground."

"Warn me before you start putting your suicidal plan into action. I need to gather up my evidence and get out of here."

Buck had looked at the smaller man, not knowing how to take the man. "But you're a federal marshal, MacGregor. Aren't you going to arrest me?"

"On what charges, Buck? I'm not aware of any federal charges against you. You haven't committed any acts of treason against the government of the United States. You haven't robbed any federal mints. You haven't assaulted any federal agents or destroyed any federal property. Hell, I personally hope you are successful in destroying this cesspool. Good day, Mr. West."

Buck stabled Drifter and went back to the hotel for a bath and shave. MacGregor hadn't told him very much as to the why of a federal marshal being in Bury; just that if he, MacGregor, was successful, another chapter in that regrettable bloody insurrection referred to as the Civil War would be closed. And perhaps a young man would finally be at peace with himself.

MacGregor had left it at that.

After cleaning up, Buck walked to Sally's house carrying a small package wrapped in brown paper. He found her working in the yard, planting flowers. She turned at the sounds of his bootheels and the jingle of his spurs and smiled at him.

Brushing off her hands, Sally asked, "Did you have a good trip?"

"Oh, yes." Buck held out the package. "Brought you something."

She waved him onto the porch and they both took chairs. She opened the package and laughed out loud. Two pounds of coffee.

"I'll grind these beans and make some coffee right now," she said. "While it's perking I'll clean up. It won't take me five minutes."

They chatted away the remainder of the morning. Sally fixed sandwiches for lunch, then the two went for a stroll around town. While resting on the cool banks of a creek, Buck said, "Sally, I want to tell you something."

She glanced at him. "Sounds serious."

"Might be. Sally, if I ever come to you and tell you to pack up and get out of town, don't question it. Just do as I say. If I ever tell you that, it's because a lot of trouble is about to pop wide open."

"If there is an Indian attack, wouldn't it be safer in town rather than outside of town?"

"It won't be Indians, Sally."

"There are children in this town, Buck," she reminded him.

"I'm aware of that."

"Are you saying the sins of the father are also on the head of the son?"

"No," Buck's reply was given slowly, after much thought. "Why would I think that?"

She touched his face with her small hand. "Who are you, Buck?"

And just before his lips touched hers, Buck said, "Smoke Jensen."

"Well, this cinches it," Richards told MacGregor. "I've got a man I can trust. You agree?"

"Oh, most assuredly," the Scotsman said. "I like the young man."

Richards gave his bookkeeper a sharp glance. Damned little sour man had never seemed to like anybody. But if MacGregor gave his OK to Buck West, then Buck was all right.

"Boss," Jerry stuck his head into the office. "Some range-rider just reported a group of old mountain men's gatherin' south and west of here."

"Mountain men?" Richards said. "That's impossible. All those people are dead."

"No, sir," Jerry respectfully disagreed with his boss. "There's still a handful of 'um around. They old, but they mean and crotchety and not to be fooled with. Dangerous old men. I've run up on 'um time to time. And Benson over to the general store reports that one was in his place 'bout three days back. Bought supplies and sich."

"Mountain men," Richards vocally mused. "Now why would those old characters be hanging around here?"

Neither Richards nor Jerry noticed the faint smile on MacGregor's face. The Scotsman now knew what Buck/Smoke was up to. And it amused him. But, he cautioned himself silently, you damn sure don't want to be around when Buck and his friends lift the lid on Pandora's Box. Best start making arrangements to pull out. It isn't going to be long.

"Don't know, boss," Jerry said. "Just thought you'd want to know about it."

"Yeah, right, Jerry. Thanks."

MacGregor watched the men leave the office. The undercover federal marshal sat down at his desk and took up his pen, dipping the point into the inkwell. He returned to his company ledger book. But he had a difficult time entering the small, precise figures. His shoulders kept shaking from suppressed laughter.

"I must keep reminding myself that I'm a lady," Sally told Buck. But the twinkle in her eyes told Buck that while a lady she might be, there were a lot of hot coals banked within.

"Aren't you going to run away, screaming in fear?" Buck asked her. "After all, I'm the murderer, Smoke Jensen."

"You took an awful chance, telling me that."

"Maybe I have some insight, too."

"Yes, I suppose you do. Now tell me about Smoke."

She listened attentively for a full ten minutes, not interrupting, letting him tell his painful story, his way. Several times during the telling he lapsed into silence, then with a sigh, he would continue.

When he had finished, she sat on the cool creek bank, her long skirt a fan of gingham around her, and

91

mentally digested all she had heard.

Finally she said, "And to think I work for those creatures." She hurled a small stone into the water. "Well, I shall tender my resignation immediately, of course."

Buck's smile was hard. "Stick around, Sally. The show's just about to begin."

"What would you do if I told you I . . . well, I am quite fond of you, Buck?"

"What would you want me to do?"

"Well," she smiled, "you might kiss me."

Just as their lips touched, a voice came from behind them. "Plumb sickenin'. Great big growed-up man a-moonin' and a-sparkin' lak some fiddle-footed kid. Disgustin'."

Buck spun around, on his feet in a crouch, his hands over the butt of his guns. His mouth dropped open.

"Shut your mouth, boy," Preacher said. "Flies is bad this time of year."

"Preacher!" Buck croaked, his voice breaking.

"It damned shore ain't Jedediah Smith," the old man said drily. "We lost him back in '35, I think it was. Either that or he got married. One and the same if'n you's to ask me."

Buck ran toward Preacher and grabbed him in a bear hug, spinning around and around with the old mountain man.

"Great Gawd Amighty!" Preacher hollered. "Put me down, you ox!"

Buck dropped the old man to the ground. His big hands on Preacher's shoulders, Buck said, "I can't believe it. I thought you were dead!"

"I damn near was, boy! Took this old body a long time to recover. Now if'n you're all done a-slobberin' all over me, we got to make some plans."

92

"How'd you find me. Preacher?"

"Hell's fire, boy! I just followed the bodies! Cain't you keep them guns of yourn in leather?"

"Come on, Preacher! Tell the truth. I know you'd rather lie, but try real hard."

"You see how unrespectful he is, Missy?" Preacher looked at Sally. "Cain't a purty thang lak you do no better than the laks of this gunslick?"

"I'm going to change him," Sally said primly. She was not certain just how to take this disreputable-looking old man, all dressed in buckskins and looking like death warmed over.

"Uh-huh," Preacher said. "That's whut that white wife of mine said, too."

"White wife!" Buck looked at him. "You never had no wife except squaws!"

"That's all you know, you pup. I married up with me a white woman that was purtier than Simone Jules Dumont's mustache."

"Heavens!" Sally muttered.

Simone Jules Dumont, also known as Madame Mustache, was either from France or a Creole from the Mississippi Delta region—it had never been proven one way or the other. She'd showed up in California during the 1849 gold rush and had soon been named head roulette croupier at the Bella Union in San Francisco. Eventually, Simone had moved on to a livelier occupation: running a gambling saloon/whorehouse at Bannack, Montana. It was there she is rumored to have taught the finer points of card dealing to Calamity Jane. And her mustache continued to grow, as did her reputation. She killed what is thought to be her first husband—a man named Carruthers—after he conned her out of a sizable amount of money. She moved on to Bodie, California, mustache in full bloom, and killed another man there when he and another footpadder tried to rob her one night. She lost most of her money in a card game on the night of September 6, 1879, and passed on through the Pearlies that same night after drinking hydrocyanic acid.

"Did you have any children from that union, Mister Preacher?" Sally asked.

"Durned if'n I know, Missy. I lit a shuck out of there one night. Walls was a-closin' in on me. I heard she took up with a minister and went back east. I teamed up with John Liver-Eatin' Johnston for a time. He lost his old woman back in '47 and went plumb crazy for a time. Called him Crow Killer. He kilt about three hundred Crows and et the livers out of 'em."

Sally turned a little green around the mouth. Buck had heard the story; he yawned.

"I didn't think crows were good to eat, Mister Preacher," Sally said.

"Not the bird, Missy," Preacher corrected. "The Indian tribe. You see, it was a bunch of Crows on the warpath that kilt Johnston's old woman. John never did lak Crows after that. Et a bunch of 'em."

"You mean he was a . . . a *cannibal*?"

"Only as fer as the liver went," Preacher said blandly. "He got to lookin' at me one night while we's a-camped in the Bitterroot. Right hongry look in his eyes. I took off. Ain't seen him since. Last I heard, old Crow Killer was a scout for the U.S. Army, over on the North Plains."

Sally sat back on the bank, averting her eyes, mumbling to herself.

"I wish you had gotten word to me that you were still alive, you old coot," Buck said.

"Couldn't. I were plumb out of it for a couple of months. By the time I could ride out of that Injun camp, Nicole and the baby was dead and buried and you was gone. I'm right sorry about Nicole and the boy, Smoke."

Buck nodded. "Better get use to calling me Buck, Preacher. You might slip up in town and that would be the end of it."

"I ain't goin' into town. Not until you git ready to make your move, that is. You wanna git a message to me, Smoke, they'll be a miserable-looking old Injun in town named Hunts-Long. Flathead. Wears a derby hat. He'll git word to me. Me and the boys was spotted last yesterday, so we'll be changin' locations." He told Buck where. "I's tole you met up with Audie." That was said with a grin.

"I thought I was seeing things. I thought he was an elf."

"He's the furrtherest thang from an elf. That little man will kill you faster than you can spit. Yessir, Smoke, you got some backup that'll be wrote up strong when they writes about the buryin' of Bury. Got Tenneysee, Audie, Phew, Nighthawk, Dupre, Deadlead, Powder Pete, Greybull, Beartooth, and Lobo. And me. Course I'm a better man than all them combined," Preacher said, in his usual modest manner. "And Matt."

"Phew?" Sally said. "Why in Heaven's name would you call a man that?"

" 'Cause he stinks, Missy."

"I know Matt. The negro."

"That's him. Ol' one-eye." Preacher stuck out his hand. "Be lookin' at you, Smoke. You take care, now." He whistled for his pony and the spotted horse trotted over. Preacher jumped on the mustang's back and was gone.

Sally looked at Buck. A load seemed to have been removed from his shoulders. His eyes were shining

95

with love as he watched the old man ride out. He seemed to stand a little taller.

He met her eyes. "It's sad. When those men are gone, a . . . time will have passed. And it will never be again."

"That is not entirely true, Smoke Jensen," Sally said.

"Oh? What do you mean?"

"You'll be here to carry on."

12

The day after seeing Preacher, Buck was witness to a scene that lent credence to what MacGregor had said about the men and women who made up the population of Bury. Buck was sitting on the board-walk in front of one of Bury's hurdy-gurdy houses, leaned back in his chair, when a man and woman and three children walked up the main street. The man and woman wore rags and the kids looked as though they had not eaten in days. The ragged little band of walkers stopped in front of the large general store. Buck drifted over that way just as the red-headed cowboy, Sam, walked over from another direction. Buck and Sam looked at each other and nodded greetings.

"Watch this," Sam said out of the corner of his mouth. "This might change your mind about the men you're working for. And the sorry people in this town."

"You get your money out of the same hand that pays me," Buck reminded him.

"But I don't have to like it . . . Smoke."

"Do I know you from somewheres else?" Buck asked.

"I was in Canon City when you and that old mountain man drew down on Ackerman and his boys. Took me awhile to put it all together. But I knowed

97

I'd seen you before."*

"Why haven't you tried to collect the bounty on my head, then?"

Sam hesitated. "I don't know," he finally admitted. "Mayhaps I'm havin' some second thoughts 'bout the way my life's been goin' up to date. And then mayhaps I just want to hang around and see the show. 'Cause I know when the time gets right, you're goin' to put on one hell of show."

"You gonna watch my back?"

"I don't know. Talk to you later. Listen to this."

The ragged emaciated-looking man was talking to the store manager. "I'm begging you, mister. Please. My kids are starving and my wife is worn out. I ain't asking nothing for myself. Just a bite of food for my wife and kids. I'll work it out for you."

The storekeeper waved his broom at the ragged man. "Get on with you. Get out of here. Go beg somewhere else."

"I'll get down on my knees and beg you, mister," the man said. He was so tired, so worn out, he was trembling.

The man who ran the leather shop next to the general store stepped out onto the boardwalk to watch the show. "What happened to you, skinny?" he called to the ragged man.

"Indians. They ambushed the wagon train we was on. We didn't have time to circle. They split us up. Most of the others died. We lost everything and have been walking for days. Brother, can you find it in your heart to give my kids and woman something to eat?"

"Only if you got the money to pay for it. If you don't, then haul your ashes on, beggar."

The man's shoulders sagged and tears began rolling

*The Last Mountain Man.

down his dusty face.

Buck could not believe what he was hearing and seeing. But he knew he could not afford to step out of character—not yet. He watched and waited.

Other shopkeepers had gathered on the boardwalk. The man who ran the apothecary shop laughed and said, "There's a joyhouse down the end of this street. Why don't you put your woman in there? Clean 'er up some and she'll make enough to get you goin' again." The gathering crowd roared with laughter.

Sam explained. "Man poisoned his partner back in Illinoise," he said. "Then stole his woman and come out here. Real nice feller. Name's Burton."

"Yeah," Sam returned the low tone.

The hotel manager stepped out. He waved his arms at the ragged little band. "You ne'er-do-wells get out of here. That little girl looks like she's got galloping consumption. No one here wants to catch that. Stir up the dust and get gone from here."

"Morgan," Sam said. "Ran a hotel in Ohio until he burned it down. Killed several sleepers. Another nice feller."

"I just don't believe the heartlessness of these people," Buck said.

"You ain't seen nothin' yet, partner," Sam said. "Stick around."

"The Lord helps those who help themselves," Reverend Necker said, appearing on the scene. "But He frowns on shirkers. Now be gone with you."

"A minister?" Buck whispered.

"About as holy as you and me," Sam said. "Come from Iowa, so he says. He's a drunk and a skirt-chaser."

The woman had gathered her children close to her

99

and was fighting back tears. The man's shoulders were slumped in defeat.

Sheriff Reese and Deputy Rogers walked up. "You vagabonds keep on moving," the sheriff ordered. "Get on with you now before I put a loop on you all and drag you out of town."

"I don't believe I'm seeing this!" Sally shouted from the fringe of the crowd. Her hot eyes found Buck and bored invisible holes into his heart. She swung her eyes back to the merchants gathered on the boardwalk. "What is the matter with you people?"

"Warn her off," Sam whispered. "You and me will get some grub and clothes for them people; give it to them on the outskirts of town. But warn her off, Buck. She's treadin' on dangerous ground."

"How?" Buck whispered.

Sam grunted. "Good question, I reckon. That lady would stand up to an Injun attack armed with a broom, I'm thinkin'."

"You people should be ashamed of yourselves!" Sally shouted. "Look at those children. *Look at them!* They're starving."

"This ain't none of your business, Miz Sally," Sheriff Reese said. "You just go on back home and tend to your knittin'."

"Well, I'll make it my business!" Sally flared, sticking her chin out and standing her ground. She looked at the ragged, starving family. "You people come with me. To my house. I'll give you all a hot meal."

"No, you won't, Miss Reynolds," the voice came from the edge of the crowd.

All heads turned to stare at Keith Stratton, mounted on a showy white horse.

"What do you mean, Mr. Stratton?" Sally asked.

"Those people are losers, Miss Reynolds," Stratton

said. "No matter what or how much one does for them, they will be begging again tomorrow. Trash. That's all they are. All they ever will be. And you don't own that house you're living in. I do. You are staying there rent-free. And you are paid to teach school, not meddle in town affairs. Now please leave."

"And if I choose to stay?" Sally asked.

"You will neither have a job, nor a place to stay," Stratton warned.

"Stratton just stepped into a pit full of rattlers," Sam projected accurately. "All dressed up in gingham."

"Yep," Buck said.

"I see," Sally said. "Will you allow me the time to gather up my personal belongings, or do you intend to seize those along with the house?"

"You're about to make a very bad mistake, Sally," Stratton informed her.

"There is quite a popular phrase out here, Mr. Stratton," Sally said. "It is said that out in the west, a person saddles their own horses and kills their own snakes."

"I'm familiar with the saying," Stratton said, his triple chins quavering as he spoke. The sunlight glinted off his diamond rings.

"Then I stand by that maxim, sir."

"A what?" Sam whispered.

"Don't ask me," Buck said.

"You're a very foolish and headstrong young woman, Miss Reynolds. But if that is your decision, then you have one hour to gather up your possessions and vacate that house."

Sally nodded and looked at the ragged family. "You people come with me."

Buck started toward Sally. She waved him back. "You have made your choice, Buck. So long as you

101

work for the other side, I do not wish to see you."

She winked at him.

Buck hid his smile, knowing then what Sally was doing. She was jeopardizing her own position in order to strengthen his own. Gal had guts, Buck thought. But where in the hell was she going to stay the night? he wondered.

"She's going to stay *where*?" Buck shouted at Sam.

Sam backed up. "Easy now, partner." He kept his hands away from his guns. "She's gonna stay down at Miss Flora's place."

"A whorehouse!"

"It wasn't my idea, Buck. It was Miss Flora's. She likes Sally 'cause Sally was always nice and polite to them, ah, ladies that work the Pink House."

"Sally Reynolds in a whorehouse!"

The red-headed cowpuncher-turned-gunslick took another step backward. The last thing in this world he wanted was for Buck to reach for those guns. Sam was fast, but Lord knows not nearabouts that fast. "Miss Flora done closed the doors to the Pink House, Buck. Shut 'er down tight. She's been wanting to pull up stakes for a year. Take her girls and head out. Stratton and them blocked that move. Made her mad. Now she's locked the doors to the Pink House. This is liable to bring things to a head 'round here, Buck."

Buck began to relax as the humor of the situation struck him. He had been told that the Big Three built the joyhouse to keep their randy gunhands happy. If Miss Flora had indeed shut the Pink House down, a lot of gunhands were going to be walking around with a short fuse.

Leave it to Sally to light the fuse.

Buck asked, "What happened to that poor family?"

"Sally give 'um a big poke of food and money enough to buy clothes and a wagon and horses. You knew she was rich, didn't you?"

"Sally? Rich?"

"Folks is. Her daddy owns a lot of factories and such back east. Her momma has money too. Stratton and Potter and Richards just might have grabbed ahold of a puma's tail this time. I hear Wiley Potter was all upset about what Stratton done today. He sent word to Sally to go on back to her little house and forget what happened. Sally told him, through Miss Flora, that she would forget only when pigs fly."

Deputy Rogers walked up, a grim look on his face. "Buck West! You go see Mr. Richards over to the office. And you, Sam, is fired. Them words come from Mr. Stratton. He's done found out about you helpin' them dirt farmers over in the flats. Git your gear and be out of town by sundown." He looked at Buck. "Move, West!"

Buck silently stared the big deputy down. With a curse, Rogers wheeled around and stalked away.

"What dirt farmers, Sam?"

"It's a big country, Buck. They's room for lots of folks. The Big Three don't object to farmers comin' in, but only if they agree to the terms set up by Potter and Stratton and Richards. If they don't, they git burnt out and run off the land. I don't hold none with the likes of that. A young couple with two little kids moved in last year. Just after I joined up. Started homesteadin'. Richards sent some of his hardcases in. When the man got his back up, Long shot him dead. Becky—that's the widder woman's name—stayed on the place, workin' it herself. I kinda helped along from time to time. I was raised on a farm in Minnesota. Guess they heard about my helpin' out."

103

Buck looked hard at the man. Could he trust him, or was this a set-up? He decided to play along, test Sam. "You stick around. I'm going to see Richards. When I'm through, we'll take a ride out to the Widow Becky's place. OK?"

"All right, Buck. I'll be at the livery."

Buck walked to the PSR offices. Richards was waiting for him. He pointed to saddlebags on the counter. "No test this time, Buck. The corporation is buying more land. Those bags contain gold dust and the contracts. Man named Gilmore is waiting for you in Challis. Get the papers signed, give him the dust, and get back here."

"Yes, sir."

Buck picked up the saddlebags and walked to the stable. Sam was waiting for him, talking with the little boy Buck had given the gold piece to. Sam grinned at Buck.

"This here is Ben. This stable is his home. His pa was kilt in a cave-in a couple of years ago. He ain't got no ma. He's a good boy. Keeps his mouth shut. And he don't like none of the Big Three. Stratton took a whip to him last year. Marked him up pretty good. Richards kicked him off the boardwalk later on. Bust a rib. He's all right, Buck."

"You go to school, Ben?" Buck asked.

"No, sir. Mister Rosten won't let me. Says I gotta work here all the time."

Ben looked to be about nine years old.

Buck nodded. He mentally added Rosten's name to his list of sorry people. "You seen an old Indian around? Wears a derby hat?"

"Hunts-Long. Yes, sir. When he's in town he camps down by the creek yonder." Ben pointed.

"You go tell Hunts-Long I said it's time. Get the word out. He'll know what you mean." Buck gave the boy some coins. Ben took off.

"We can't be seen leaving town together, Sam. Where do you want to meet?"

"Crick just south of town, 'bout four mile. I'll meet you there in a couple of hours."

Buck nodded. "If you playin' a game, Sam, workin' for the other side, you'll never live to see the game finished."

"I believe you, Buck. Or Smoke. No games. I'm done with that. See you at the crick."

Buck watched the cowboy ride out. He wondered if he was going to have to kill him.

13

Buck took his time saddling Drifter. He watched the old Flathead, Hunts-Long, ride out. He was conscious of Little Ben looking at him.

"You know Miss Flora, boy?"

"Yes, sir. Down to the Pink House."

"After I'm gone, you walk down there and tell Miss Sally Reynolds I said to keep her head down. She'll know what I mean. You got that?"

"Yes, sir. Mister Buck? Sam's a nice feller. He ain't no real gunhand. He got backed into it."

"How's that, Ben?"

"Story is—I heard some men talkin'—a deputy over in Montana Territory pushed Sam hard one day. Sam tried to get out of it, but the deputy drew on him. Sam was faster. Kilt the man and had to take the hoot-owl trail." The boy grinned. "Sam's sweet on Miz Becky."

"Sam told me he was from Minnesota."

"Yes, sir. That's what I heard, too. Sam wants to go back to farmin', way I heared it."

"A lot of us would like to be doin' something other than what we're doin', Ben. But a man gets his trail stretched out in front of him, sometimes you just got to ride it to trail's end, whether you like it or not."

"You be careful, Mister Buck."

"See you, boy."

Buck rode out easy. He could feel . . . *something* in the air. A feeling of tension, he thought. And he wondered about it. The pot was about to boil over in Bury, and Buck didn't know what had caused the fire to get too hot. But he knew that sometimes just the slightest little push could turn over a cart—if the contents weren't stacked right.

A mile out of town, Buck cut off the road and reined up, hidden in the timber. He waited for half an hour. No riders passed him. He rode out of the timber, heading for the creek.

"Buck, this here is Becky," Sam said. He was trying very hard not to grin, and not being very successful.

Becky's hair was as red as Sam's, her tanned face pretty and freckled across the nose. She was a slender lady, but Buck could sense a solid, no-nonsense quiet sort of strength about her. Two red-headed kids stood close by her. A boy and a girl. About four and six, Buck guessed. They grinned shyly up at Buck. He winked at them and they both giggled.

Buck took the lady's hand and was not surprised to find it hard and callused from years of hard work.

After talking with Becky and the kids for a few moments, Buck took Sam aside. "You stay here with her, Sam. Until I get back from Challis. Don't be surprised if you spot some old mountain men while I'm gone. I'm going to swing by their camp and tell them I'm just about ready to strike. I'll tell them about your lady friend here, too. They'll probably ride by to see if they can get her anything. And they'll be by. They don't hold with men who hurt womenfolks."

"Who are your friends, Buck? These mountain

107

men, I mean?"

Sam stood open-mouthed as Buck reeled off the names of some of the most famous mountain men of all time. Sam finally blinked and said, "Those are some of the meanest old codgers that ever forked a bronc."

"Yeah," Buck said with a grin as he swung into the saddle. "Ain't they?"

He waved good-bye to Becky and the kids and pointed Drifter's nose south. A mile from Becky's cabin, Buck turned straight east, toward the new camp of Preacher and his friends. Even Buck, knowing what to expect, drew up short at the sight that soon confronted him.

Greybull and Beartooth were wrestling. Dupre was fiddling a French song while Nighthawk and Tenneysee were dancing. Together. Audie was standing on a stump, reciting pretty poetry to the others.

"I hate to break this up," Buck said.

"Then don't!" Preacher said. "Jist sit your cayuse and listen and learn. Go ahead, Audie. Tell us some more about that there Newton."

"*Isaac* Newton, you ignorant reprobate! I was merely stating Sir Newton's theory that to every action there is always opposed an equal reaction: or, the mutual actions of two bodies upon each other are always equal, and directed to contrary parts."

"Then direct it to him," Buck said, pointing at Preacher. "Cause he sure is contrary."

Audie looked pained while the others laughed. He glowered at Buck. "If I had you in a classroom I'd take a hickory stick to the seat of your pants, young man."

"I don't know nothing about Newton," Buck said, still sitting on Drifter. "But I did like that poetry. Can you say some more of that?"

"But of course, young outlaw called Smoke," Audie said with a wave of his hand. "Dismount and gather around."

Dupre had stopped his fiddling, Nighthawk and Tenneysee their dancing, Greybull and Beartooth their wrestling.

" 'I came to the place of my youth'," Audie said, " 'and cried, The friends of my youth, where are they? And echo answered, Where are they?' "

"That don't make no damn sense," Phew said.

"And it don't even rhyme," Deadlead growled.

"It doesn't have to rhyme to be poetry!" Audie said. "I have told you heathens that time and again."

"Say something that's purty," Preacher said.

"Yeah, that fits us'ns," Powder Pete said.

"What a monumental task you have verbally laid before me," Audie said. "Very well. Let me think for a moment."

"And I don't reckon it has to rhyme," Matt said.

Audie smiled. He said, " 'And in that town a dog was found. As many dogs there be, both mongrel, puppy, whelp, and hound, And curs of low degree. The dog, to gain some private ends, Went mad, and bit the man. The man recovered of the bite, The dog it was that died.' " Still smiling, Audie stepped off the stump and walked off, leaving the old mountain men to scratch their heads and ponder what he'd just said.

"Is he callin' us a bunch of *dogs*?" Lobo asked.

"I don't think so," Preacher said.

Deadlead looked at Nighthawk. "What do you think about it, Nighthawk?"

"Ummm."

Buck's ride to Challis was uneventful. He found the man named Gilmore, completed his business, and headed back. When he rode into Bury, past Miss Flora's Pink House, he noticed the front door was closed, a hand-lettered sign hanging from a string. *Closed*, the sign read. Smiling, Buck rode to the PSR office and handed the receipt to MacGregor. The Scotsman had a worried look on his now-more-than-ever dour face.

"What's wrong?" Buck asked.

"New territorial governor was just named. It wasn't Potter. He's fit to be tied."

"You knew it wouldn't be all along, didn't you?"

"I had a rather strong suspicion."

"Now what?"

"I don't know. I haven't got enough evidence to bring any of the Big Three to court and make it stick. The Big Three violate a number of *moral* laws. But they run their own businesses on the up and up—so far as I've been able to find out. They have committed murder—either themselves or by hiring it out—but since this town, and all the people in it, belong to the Big Three, no one will talk. But there is a sour, rancid feeling hanging in the air, Buck, Smoke—what *is* your real name?"

"Kirby."

MacGregor nodded absently. "I gather those mountain men in the timber are friends of yours?"

"Preacher helped raise me. I know most of the others." He named them.

MacGregor chuckled. "Old bastards!" he said, with no malice in the profanity. "Did you know Audie is the holder of several degrees?"

"Yes. How did you know about that?"

"Oh, ever since I came out here, fifteen years ago, I have maintained a journal of sorts. I should like to take all those pages and turn them into a book someday. A book about mountain men. I've talked with many of them. But my God, they *lie* so much. I can't tell what is truth and what is fiction."

"I've discovered that most of what they say is true."

"Really now, Smoke! A human being cannot successfully fight a grizzly bear and win!"

"Negro Matt fought a mountain lion with his bare hands and killed it. Preacher fought a bear up on the North Milk in Canada and killed it. Jedediah Smith fought a grizzly and killed it—by himself. Bear chewed off one of his ears, though. Shoo Fly Miller had a grizzly bear for a pet. Those old boys are still about half hoss, half alligator."

"My word!" MacGregor said.

"Stick around, Mac," Buck said cheerfully. "If you live through what's coming up shortly, you can write the final chapter to the lives of the mountain men."

It was going sour, Buck thought, walking from the PSR offices back to his hotel. He could sense it; an almost tangible sensation. The gunhands that were constantly in view were behaving in a surly manner. Cursing more and drinking more openly. Buck noticed a distinct lack of kids playing on the boardwalks and streets. He noticed a couple of loaded-down wagons parked in front of the general store.

Buck stopped in front of a saloon and asked the scar-faced Joiner, "What's going on?"

"Two schoolteachers and their families pullin' out. Didn't like the way Miz Sally was treated. The boss is some sore, let me tell you."

Buck smiled.

Joiner looked sourly at him. "You find something funny about that, West?"

"Just that a man can't push some women, is all."

Joiner grunted. It was obvious to Buck that he was

111

looking for a fight. And Buck wasn't.

When Joiner saw that Buck wasn't going to fight, he said, "There can't be much sand to your bottom, boy."

Buck met him eye to eye. "If you want to get a shovel and start digging for that sand, Joiner, feel free to do so. But I'd suggest you make one stopover first for a little digging."

"Oh? And where's that?"

"Boot Hill." Buck turned and walked on up the street. As he turned, his right side blocked to Joiner's view, Buck slipped the hammer thong off his .44.

He could feel Joiner's eyes boring into his back as he walked.

"Buck West!" Joiner shouted. "Turn and fight, you tinhorn!"

Buck heard Joiner's hand as his palm struck the wooden grips of his pistol.

Turning, Buck drew, cocked, and fired, all in one fluid motion. Joiner's pistol clattered to the wooden boardwalk as the .44 slug from Buck's gun hit him squarely in the center of the chest. Joiner staggered backward, grabbed at a wooden chair for support, missed the arm of the chair, and sat down heavily on the boardwalk, one hand supporting himself, holding himself up, the other hand covering the hole in his chest.

"You bassard!" Joiner hissed at Buck.

"You pushed me, Joiner," Buck reminded the man.

Joiner groaned and let himself slump to the boards.

Burton ran out of the apothecary shop, crossed the street, and knelt by the dying Joiner. When he looked up at Buck, his face was flushed with hate. "If you're so damned good with a gun, why didn't you just shoot the gun out of his hand? You didn't have to kill him."

"I ain't dead!" Joiner protested weakly.

"You ain't far from it," Burton told him.

"Get me a preacher!" Joiner said.

"He'd probably do you more good than a doctor," Burton agreed.

Buck punched out the spent brass and slid a live round into the chamber. He dropped the empty brass to the dirt of the street just as the sounds of a carriage approaching rattled through the air. The carriage *whoaed* up beside the blood-slicked boardwalk and the tall gunhand standing impassively over the dying Joiner.

"Oh, my word!" the woman seated in the carriage said.

"Help me, Miz Janey!" Joiner cried.

A group of Cornish miners in town from their work at a nearby silver mine, gathered around, beer mugs in callused hands.

"The bloke's nearly done," one immigrant from Cornwall observed. "Shall we sing him a fare-thee-well, mates?"

"Aye. Let's."

A half-dozen voices were raised in song, drunkenly offering up a hymn.

A jig dancer from the hurly-gurly in front of which Joiner lay dying stepped out. "Can I have your pockets, love?" she asked Joiner.

"Get away with you!" Reverend Necker said, running up. "You filthy whore!"

"Careful, Bible-thumper," the jig dancer said. "Or I'll tell everybody where you was the other evenin'."

Necker flushed and bent down over the dying Joiner.

"He kilt me!" Joiner said, pointing a trembling finger at Buck.

"Damn sure did," Necker said.

Buck raised his eyes to look squarely at the woman

seated in the fancy carriage.

Janey met the tall young man's direct stare.

The elegantly dressed woman flushed as Buck's eyes stared directly at her.

"Save me, Preacher!" Joiner groaned. "I don't wanna go to Hell. I got a family to take care of."

"Where are they, son?" Necker asked. He looked at the blood on his hands. Joiner's blood. "Yukk!" Necker said.

"Damned if I know," Joiner said. Then he closed his eyes and did the world the greatest favor men of his ilk could do. He died.

Janey stared at Buck. Her eyes widened as Buck smiled. She watched as Buck turned and walked away.

It couldn't be! she thought. That was impossible. Kirby was back in Missouri, probably working that damned hardscrabble farm.

But she knew the man who had killed Joiner. She knew him. It was her brother.

14

Janey stood in her bedroom, absently gazing out the window. So Buck West was really Kirby Jensen, aka Smoke. She laughed, but the laugh was totally void of mirth. She suddenly remembered all the good times they'd shared as children, back in Missouri. It had been a hard life, but despite that, there had been plenty of love to go around. Never enough money for nice things, but none of them had gone hungry.

"Crap!" Janey said, turning away from the window. She didn't know what to do. The gunfighter was blood kin, but Janey felt no warmth toward him. She looked around her. Damned if she was going to give all this up for a man she hadn't seen since he was a snot-nosed kid tryin' to farm forty rocky acres with a damned ol' mule.

She walked downstairs, searching for Josh.

"Gone, ma'am," the negro houseman informed her.

"Gone, where?"

"Up to the north range to inspect the herds, ma'am. Won't be back for several days."

"Bull-droppings!" Janey blurted.

The houseman's eyes widened.

"Thank you, Thomas," Janey said. "That will be all.

Now she sure didn't know what to do.

MacGregor ceased his pacing, his mind made up.

He would not leave Bury, as had been his original plan. He would stick it out here. If Buck West, aka Smoke Jensen, was successful in his plan, what a book that would make! And, the Scotsman smiled grimly, he could close the federal pages on Potter, Stratton, and Richards.

"He's really the outlaw Smoke?" Flora asked Sally.

"He's Smoke Jensen, but he's no outlaw," Sally told the gathering of joy-girls.

"We can't get out of town, Miss Sally," Rosa said. "The little boy, Ben, says Potter and Stratton gave orders to that nasty Rosten not to rent us wagons or horses. We're stuck."

Sally nodded. As Josh Richards had once explained to her, the Pink House was one of the best constructed buildings in town. The two-story structure was built of logs, with excellent craftsmanship in the construction, with carefully fitted corners. Instead of a mixture of clay and moss filling the chinks, solid mortar had been used. With a little rearranging of furniture, the house could easily withstand any stray bullets.

"All right, ladies," Sally said. "Here's what we'll do . . ."

"What's happening!" Deputy Rogers said. "I don't understand none of it. It's like . . . it's like ever'thang was just fine one day, and the next day it's all haywire!"

Sheriff Dan Reese knew what was happening, but he didn't feel like explaining it to this big dummy standing before him. He'd seen boom towns go sour before. And he knew that sometimes a feller could skin the clabber off the top and salvage the milk. Not often, but sometimes.

But he had a sinking feeling it was too damn late

116

for Bury.

"Shut up, Rogers," he said. He looked at his other deputies, Weathers and Payton. "You men check them shotguns and rifles. Git over to the store and stock up on shells. I don't know why, but something tells me everything that's happenin' is the fault of that Buck West. Damn his eyes!"

"So we is gonna do what?" Payton asked. Like Rogers, Payton was no mental giant.

"I think the bosses is gonna tell us to kill him."

Potter turned from the second-floor window of the PSR offices to look at Stratton. "You feel it?" he asked.

"Yes," Stratton said with a sigh. "Whatever *it* is."

"I had the territorial governorship in the palm of my hand," Potter said. "And suddenly, for no reason, I lose it. Why? A seemingly intelligent, reasonable young woman, a very capable schoolteacher, suddenly falls for a gunslick. Why? And now I discover that Buck West—or whatever his name is—is buddy-buddy with Sam, and Sam is sharing the blankets with a squatter. What's happening around here?"

"Don't forget the mountain men gathering up in the deep timber."

"That's right."

The two men looked at each other and suddenly their brains began to click and hum in unison.

"Mountain men helped raise Kirby Jensen," Stratton said.

"We've all heard the rumors that Preacher wasn't killed," Potter said.

"All our troubles started when Buck West arrived in town."

The men sent a flunky for Sheriff Dan Reese.

117

"Anybody have any idee whatever happened to old Maurice Leduc?" Deadlead asked.

The mountain men were camped openly and brazenly about two miles outside of Bury. They knew their reputation had preceded them, and they likewise knew that none of the Big Three's gunhands were about to attack the camp. For one thing, they held the vantage point—the crest of a low hill. For another, no twenty-five cowboys-turned-gunhands were about to attack a dozen old hardbitten mountain men; especially not the most notorious bunch of mountain men to ever prowl the high lonesome. No matter that none of the mountain men would ever see seventy years of age again. That had nothing to do with it. Even at seventy, most of them could still outshoot and outfight men half their age.

Lobo said, "Last I heard, ol' Leduc come back up to near Bent's fort and built hisself a cabin; him and a teenage Mex gal. Took up gardenin'." That was said very contemptuously.

"Hale's far!" Powder Pete said. "That was back in '58."

"Wal, what year is this here we're in?" Dupre asked.

"Oh . . . 'bout '75, I reckon," Tenneysee said.

"You don't say," Greybull said. "My, time does git away from a man, don't it?"

"If that is the case," Audie said. "And I will admit that I don't even know what year it is, not really, I was born seventy-one years ago."

"And got uglier every year," Preacher said.

"You should talk. You're so ugly you could pose for totem poles."

"I 'member the furst time I seen one of the things," Phew said. "Up in Washington Territory. Like to have plumb scared me out of my 'skins."

118

"That'd probably been a good thing for all concerned," Matt said. "Least you'd a took a bath then. You ain't been out of them skins in fifty year."

"I wish Smoke would git things a-smokin' down yonder," Beartooth said. "I'm a-cravin' a mite of action."

"He'll start stirrin' it up in a day or three," Preacher opined. "And then we'll all have all the action we can handle. Bet on it."

"Reckon whut he's a-doin' down there?" Lobo asked.

"Probably tryin' to spark that schoolmarm," Preacher said. "He's shore stuck on her."

"What do you mean, I can't come in?" Buck said, standing on the front porch of the Pink House.

"Buck," Sally's voice came through the closed door. "You'd better get out of town. Little Ben just slipped up to the back door and told us Sheriff Reese and his deputies are looking for you. Word just drifted into town that you're Smoke Jensen."

So the cat was out of the bag. Fine. He was getting tired of being Buck West. "You . . . ladies have plenty of food and water?"

"Enough for a month-long siege. Go on, Buck."

"Call me Smoke."

15

Smoke slipped around the side of the Pink House and into the weed-grown alley in the rear. He carefully picked his way toward the rear of the stable. He felt sure the front of the stable would be watched.

For the first time since he had arrived in Bury, the town was silent. No wagons rattled up and down the streets. No riders moving in and out of town. No foot traffic to be seen in Bury. A tiny dust devil spun madly up the main street, picking up bits of paper as it whirled away.

Smoke slipped from outhouse to outhouse, both hammer thongs off his .44s.

Reese and his deputies apparently believed Smoke would not take to the alleys, but instead stroll right down the center of the main street, spurs jingling, like some tinhorn kid who fancied himself a gunhand. But Smoke had been properly schooled by Preacher, whose philosophy was thus: if you're outnumbered, circle around 'hind 'em and ambush the hell out of 'em. Ain't no such thang as a fair fight, boy. Just a winner and a loser.

Smoke didn't want to open the dance just yet. He was in a very bad position, being on foot and armed with only his short guns.

And he was still about a block and a half from the

120

stable. His eyes picked up the shape of a small boy, frantically and silently waving his arms. Little Ben. Smoke returned the wave. Ben disappeared into the stable and returned seconds later, leading a saddled and ride-ready Drifter. Smoke grinned. Drifter must have taken a liking to Little Ben, for had he not, the stallion would have stomped the boy to death.

"Jensen!" The harshly spoken word came from his right, from the shadows of an alley.

Out of the corner of his eye, Smoke could see the young man had not drawn his pistol. The cowboy was a PSR rider, but Smoke did not know his name.

Smoke slowly turned, facing the young rider. "Back away, cowboy," Smoke stated softly. "Just walk back up the alley and no one will ever have to know. If you draw on me, I'll kill you. Turn around and you'll live. How about it?"

"That thirty thousand dollars looks almighty good to me, Jensen," the puncher replied, his hands hovering over his low-tied guns. "Start me up a spread with that."

"You'll never live to work it," Smoke warned him. Ben was slowly leading Drifter up the alley.

"Says you!" the cowboy sneered.

"What's your name, puncher?"

"Jeff Siddons. Why?"

"So I'll know what to put on your grave marker." Jeff flushed. "You gonna draw or talk?"

"I'd rather not draw at all," Smoke again tried to ease out of the fight.

"You yellow scum!" Jeff said. "Draw!" His hands dipped downward.

Jeff's hands had just touched the wooden handles of his guns when he felt a terrible crushing double blow to his chest. The young cowboy staggered backward, falling heavily against the side of the building.

Smoke was already turning away from the dying cowboy as light faded in Jeff's eyes. "Ain't no human man that fast!" Jeff spoke his last words, sitting in his own dusty blood.

Smoke looked back at the dying cowboy. "Just remember to tell Saint Peter this wasn't my idea."

But he was talking to a dead man.

He heard the drum of bootheels on the boardwalk, all running in his direction. He turned just as a voice called out, "Hold it, Jensen!"

Smoke ducked in back of the building just as a shot rang out, the bullet knocking a fist-sized chunk of wood out of the building. Smoke dropped to one knee and fired two fast shots around the side of the building, then he was up and running toward Ben and Drifter, ignoring the howl of pain behind him and in the alley. At least one of his snap shots had struck home.

"That damned little stable boy's helpin' Jensen!" a man's voice yelled. "I'll take a horsewhip to that little son of a bitch!"

Smoke reached Ben and Drifter. "Run to Miss Flora's, Ben. Them women won't let anything happen to you. Run, boy, run!"

Ben took off as if pursued by the devil. Smoke mounted up. His saddlebags were bulging, so Ben must have transferred a lot of his gear from the packs normally borne by the pack animal. He looked back over his shoulder. Sheriff Reese was leading a running gang of men. And they weren't far behind Smoke.

"Hold up there, Jensen!" Reese yelled, just as Smoke urged Drifter forward and cut into the alley where the dead cowboy lay. Reese lifted a double-barreled coach gun and pulled the trigger. The buckshot tore a huge hole in the corner of the building.

Drifter leaped ahead and charged through the alley,

coming out on the main street. Smoke turned his nose north for a block and then whipped into another alley, coming out behind Reese and his men. Smoke had reloaded his Colts and now, with the reins in his teeth, a Colt in each hand, he charged the knot of gunslicks headed by Sheriff Reese.

"I want that thirty thousand!" a man yelled. Smoke recognized the man as Jerry, from back at the trading post.

"Hell with you!" Reese said. "I want that—" He turned at the sound of drumming hooves. "Jesus Christ!" he hollered, looking at the mean-eyed stallion bearing down on him.

The charging stallion struck one gunhand, knocking the man down, the man falling under Drifter's steel-shod hooves. The gunnie screamed, the cry cut off as Drifter's hooves pounded the man's face into pulp.

Reese had jumped out of the way of the huge midnight black horse with the killer-cold yellowish eyes, losing his shotgun as he leaped. One of Drifter's hooves struck the sheriff's thigh, bringing a howl of pain and a hat-sized bruise on the man's leg. Reese rolled on the ground, yelling in pain.

"You squatter-lovin' son!" Jerry screamed at Smoke, bringing up a .45.

Smoke leveled his left-hand .44 and shot the man between the eyes.

As blood splattered, the foot-posse broke up, fear taking over. Men ran in all directions.

Smoke urged Drifter on, galloping up the alley and once more entering the main street. He looped the reins loosely around the saddlehorn and screamed like an angry cougar, the throaty scream, almost identical to a real cougar's warcry, chilling the shopowners who were huddling behind closed doors. Stratton, Potter, and Richards had promised them a safe town and lots of easy money; they hadn't said anything about a wild man riding a horse that looked like it came straight out of the pits of Hell.

Preacher sat straight up on his blankets. He slapped one knee and cackled as the gunshots drifted out of Bury. The shots were followed by the very faint sounds of a big mountain lion screaming.

"Hot damn, boys!" Preacher hollered. "Somebody finally grabbed holt of Smoke's tail and give 'er a jerk. Bet by Gawd they'll wish they hadn't a done it."

"He a-havin' all the fun!" Beartooth gummed the words.

"They's plenty to go around," Lobo growled. "When he needs us, he'll holler."

"Ummm," said Nighthawk.

"How eloquently informative," said Audie.

Leaning close to Drifter's neck, presenting a low profile, Smoke charged up the main street. He was not going to shoot up the town, for he did not want to harm any woman or child. He had made up his mind that he was going to give the shopkeepers and the storeowners and their families a chance to pull out. But he was doing that for the sake of the kids only. To hell with the adults; man or woman, they knew who they worked for. One was as bad as the other.

Ten minutes later, Smoke had reined up and dismounted in the camp of the mountain men.

"Howdy, son!" Preacher said. "You been havin' yourself a high old time down there, huh?"

"That's one way of putting it," Smoke said, putting one heavily muscled arm around the old man's wang-leather-tough shoulders.

"You grinnin' like a chicken-eatin' dog, boy,"

Preacher said. "What you got a-rattlin' 'round in 'at head of yourn?"

Smoke looked at Powder Pete. "You got any dynamite with you?"

"Only time I been without any was when them durned Lakotas caught me up near the Canadian border and wanted to skin me. Since I was somewhat fond of my hide, I were naturally disinclined to part with it."

Smoke laughed aloud, and the laughter felt good. He felt as though he was back home, which, in a sense, he was. "What happened?"

"The chief had a daughter nobody wanted to bed down with," Powder Pete said, disgust in his voice. "Homeliest woman I ever seen. 'At squaw could cause a whirlwind to change directions. The chief agreed to let me live if'n I'd share Coyote Run's blankets. How come she got that name was when she was born the chief had a pet coyote. Coyote took one look at her and run off. Never did come back. 'At's homely, boy. I spent one winter with Coyote Run, up in the MacDonald Range, on the Flathead. Come spring, I told 'at chief he might as well git his skinnin' knife out, 'cause I couldn't stand no more of Coyote Run. Chief said he didn't know how I'd stood it this long. Told me to take off. I been carryin' dynamite ever since. Promised mysalf if'n I ever got in another bind lak 'at 'air, I'd blow mysalf up. Whut you got in mind, Smoke?"

"One road leading into and out of Bury."

Powder Pete and the other mountain men grinned. They knew then what was rattlin' around in Smoke's head.

"If you men will, find the best spots to block the road to coach and carriage travel. Set your charges. I'm going to give those who want to leave twenty-four

125

hours to do so. I want the kids out of that town. I'd prefer the women to leave as well, but from what I've been able to see and hear, most of the women are just as low-down as their men."

"Simmons's old woman is," Dupre said. "I knowed her afore. Plumb trash."

"I still want to give them a chance to leave," Smoke said. "And I especially want Sally and the women in the Pink House out, along with MacGregor and Little Ben. The rest of the townspeople can go to hell."

Deadlead and Greybull picked up their rifles. Deadlead said, "Us'n and Matt and Tenneysee will block the horse trails out of town. Rest of ya'll git busy."

"Preacher," Powder Pete said, "you take the fur end of town. I'll scout this end. I'll hook up with you in a couple hours and plant the charges."

"Done." Preacher moved out.

"I shall make the announcement to the good citizens of Bury," Audie said. "My articulation is superb and my voice carries quite well."

"Yeah," Phew said. "Like a damned ol' puma with his tail hung up in a b'ar trap. Grates on my nerves when you git to hollerin'."

Audie ignored him. "Considering the mentality of those who inhabit that miserable village, I must keep this as simple as possible. Therefore, the Socratean maieutic method of close and logical reasoning must be immediately discarded."

"Umm," Nighthawk said.

"Whut the hell did you say?" Lobo growled. "Sounded like a drunk Pawnee. Gawdamnit, you dwarf, cain't you speak plain jist once in a while?"

"Rest your gray cells, you hulking oaf," Audie responded. "I'm thinking."

"Wal, thank to yoursalf, you magpie!"

126

"Silence, you cretin!"

Smoke let them hurl taunts and insults back and forth; they had been doing it for fifty-odd years and were not about to quit at this stage of the game. He turned to face the direction of Bury.

He would give them more of a chance than they had given his brother or father. Ever so much more of a chance than they had given his baby son and his wife, Nicole. Ever so much more.

He let hate consume him as he recalled that awful day. . . .

He had made a wide circle of the cabin, staying in the timber back of the creek, and slipped up to the cabin. Inside the cabin, although Smoke did not as yet know it, the outlaw Canning had taken a blanket and smothered Baby Arthur to death. Nicole had been brutally raped, and then her throat had been crushed. Canning scalped the woman, tying her bloody hair to his belt. He then skinned a breast, thinking he would tan the hide and make himself a nice tobacco pouch.

Kid Austin had gotten sick watching Canning's callousness. He walked outside to vomit.

Another outlaw, Grissom, walked out the front of the cabin. Grissom felt something was wrong. He sensed movement behind him and reached for his gun. Smoke shot him dead.

"Behind the house!" Felter yelled.

Another of the PSR riders had been dumping his bowels in the outhouse. He struggled to pull up his pants and push over the door at the same time. Smoke shot him twice in the belly and left him to die on the craphouse floor.

Kid Austin, caught in the open, ran for the banks

of the creek. Just as he jumped, Smoke fired, the lead taking the Kid in the buttocks, entering the right cheek and tearing out the left.

Smoke waited behind a woodpile, the big Sharps buffalo rifle Preacher had given him in his hands. He watched as something came sailing out the open back door. His dead baby son bounced on the earth.

The outlaws inside the cabin taunted Smoke, telling in great detail of raping Nicole. Smoke lined up the Sharps and pulled the trigger. A PSR rider began screaming in pain.

Canning and Felter ran out the front of the cabin, hightailing it for the safety of the timber. In the creek, Kid Austin crawled upstream, crying in pain and humiliation.

Another of the PSR riders exited the cabin, leaving one inside. He got careless and Smoke took him alive.

When he came to his senses, Smoke had stripped him, staked him out over an anthill, and poured honey all over him.

It took him a long time to die.

Smoke buried his wife and son amid a colorful profusion of wild flowers, stopping often to wipe away the tears.

16

"What are you thinking, young man?" Audie asked.

"About what Potter and Stratton and Richards ordered done to my wife and son."

"Preacher told us. That was a terrible, terrible thing. But don't allow revenge to destroy you."

"When this is over, Audie, it's over. Not until."

"I understand. I have been where you are. I lost my wife, a Bannock woman, and two children to white trappers. Many many years ago."

"Did you find the men who did it?"

"Oh, yes," Audie smiled grimly. "I found them." Smoke did not have to ask the outcome.

"There will always be men who rise to power on the blood and pain of others, Smoke," the former-school-teacher-turned-mountain-man said. "Unfortunate, certainly, but a fact, perhaps a way, of life."

"The people who run the shops in that town can leave," Smoke said. "Even though I know they are, in their own way, as bad as Potter, Stratton, and Richards. I'll let them go, if they'll just go."

"They won't," Audie prophesied. "For most of them, this is the end of the trail. Behind them lies their past, filled with crime and pettiness. For most of them, all that waits behind them is prison—or a rope. Theirs is a mean, miserable existence." He waved his hand at the mountain men. "We, all us, remember when that town was built. We sat back and watched those dreary dregs of society arrive. We have all watched good people travel through, look around them, and continue on their journey. I, for one, will be glad to see that village razed and returned to the earth."

Audie walked away. About three and a half feet tall physically, about six and a half feet of man and mind and courage.

Smoke sat back on his bootheels and wondered what razed meant.

He'd have to remember to ask Sally. She'd know. And with that thought, another problem presented itself to Smoke's mind. Sally. He knew he cared a lot for the woman—more than he was willing to admit— but what did he have to offer someone like her? When news of what he planned to do to Bury reached the outside, Smoke Jensen would be the most wanted man in the west. Not necessarily in terms of reward money, for if he had his way, Potter, Stratton, and Richards would be dead and in the ground, but more in terms of reputation. A hundred, five hundred, a thousand gunhawks would be looking for him to make a reputation.

Back to the valley where Nicole and Baby Arthur were buried?

No. No, for even if Sally was willing to come with him, he couldn't go back there. Too many old memories would be in the way. He would return to the valley for his mares; he wanted to do that. Then push on and get the Appaloosa, Seven.

Then . . . ?

He didn't know. He would like to ranch and raise horses. And farm. Farming was in his blood and he had always loved the land. A combination horse and cattle ranch and farm? Why not? That was very rare

130

in the west—almost unheard of—but why not?

Would Sally be content with that? A woman of class and education and independence and wealth? Well, he'd never know until he asked her. But that would have to wait. He'd ask her later. If he lived, that is.

Deputy Rogers was the first to report back to Potter and Stratton and Sheriff Reese. Josh Richards was still out in the field; he knew nothing of the true identity of Buck West. Not yet.

"North road's blocked 'bout three miles out of town," Rogers reported. "An' I mean blown all to hell. Brought a landslide down four-five hundred feet long."

Deputy Payton galloped up and dismounted. "South road's blocked by a landslide. A bad one. Ain't nothing gonna get through there for a long time. They's riflemen stuck up all around the town, watchin' the trails. Old mountain men, looks like."

"I should have put it all together," Stratton said with a sigh. "I should have known when that damn Jensen came ridin' in, bold as brass. Should have known that's who it was."

"What are we going to do, Keith?" Wiley Stratton asked.

"Wait and find out what Jensen wants. Hell, what else can we do?"

Audie had made himself a megaphone out of carefully peeled bark. He had stationed himself on a ridge overlooking the town of Bury.

"Attention below!" Audie called. "Residents of Bury, Idaho Territory, gather in the street and curb your tongues."

"Do what with a tongue?" Deputy Rogers asked.

"Don't talk," Stratton said.

"Oh."

"Armageddon is nigh," Audie called. "Your penurious and evil practices must cease. *Will* cease—immediately. The women and the children will be allowed to leave. You have twenty-four hours to vacate and walk out with what meager possessions you can carry on your backs. Follow the flats south to Blue Meadows. Where you go from there is your own concern. Twenty-four hours. After that, the town of Bury will be destroyed."

"What's that about arms?" Dan Reese asked.

"Armageddon," Reverend Necker said. "Where the final battle will be fought between good and evil." He looked around him. "Has anybody got a jug? I need a drink."

"I ain't gonna hoof my tootsies nowhere," Louise Rosten said. "They's wild savages out there."

"Just head straight across the flats toward the east," her husband told her. "They's a settlement 'bout thirty miles over yonder. Pack up the kids and git gone. Hell, you can outshoot me."

"Hunts-Long and his Flatheads will escort the women and children to safety," Audie's voice once more rang out over the town. "They'll be waiting on the east side of the creek. You have twenty-four hours. This will be my last warning to you."

"I ain't travelin' with no damned greasy Injuns!" Veronica Morgan said. "I ain't leavin' the hotel."

Her husband looked at her. "Get those snot-nosed brats of yours and get out. I'm tired of looking at your ugly face and listening to those brats squall."

Veronica spat in her husband's face and wheeled about, stalking back to the hotel.

"Potter! Stratton! Richards!" Smoke's voice boomed through the bark-made megaphone. "This is Smoke Jensen. I'm giving you a better chance than

132

you gave my pa, my brother, and my wife and son."

None of the town's residents had to ask what Smoke was talking about. They all, to a person, knew. They knew the town was built on stolen gold and Jensen blood. They all knew the whole bloody, tragic story. And they had consented to live with that knowledge.

Stratton's heavy jowls quivered with rage and fear. He turned his little piggy eyes to Potter. "Now what?" he demanded.

"Just stay calm and keep your senses about you, man," Potter said. "Look at facts. We've a hundred and fifty men in this town. Thirty of them are hardcases drawing fighting pay. Josh is out there," he waved his hand, "with fifteen or twenty other gunhands. We're up against a handful of old men and one smart-aleck gunhawk who is too sure of himself. We've both known Hunts-Long for years. He's a peaceful, trusting Indian and so is his tribe. Send the women and kids out and we'll make ready for a siege. The stage is due in three days. We'll have someone there to meet it, turn it around, and get the Army in here from the fort. Then we'll hang Smoke Jensen and his damned old mountain men and be done with it once and for all."

Stratton and the others visibly relaxed. Sure, they thought. That was a damn good plan. Some of them began to laugh at how easy it would be. Soon all those gathered in the street were laughing and slapping one another on the back. The women were cackling and the men hoo-hawing.

"Sounds lak they havin' a celebration down thar," Lobo said. "Wush they'd let us in on it."

"They're thinking about the stage," Smoke said. "If they could turn it around with a message, they could get the Army in here and chase us all the way to

133

Canada."

"Les' we had someone down thar to meet it with a story," Phew said.

Smoke smiled at that. "That's what we'll do then."

"Now what?" Dupre said.

"We give them twenty-four hours, just like I promised."

"I can't help but feel sorry for the kids," Buck said.

"There isn't a child down there under ten or eleven years of age," Audie observed, watching through binoculars. "They are past their formative years; or very close to it. They are just smaller versions of their parents."

The sun had been up for an hour and the women and children of Bury were moving out. On foot. Had Smoke and the mountain men been able to hear the comments of the men, it would have left no doubt in any of their minds.

"I shore am glad to see that bitchin' woman clear out," Hallen said. "Hope I never see her again."

Morgan watched his wife—common law, since each of them was still married, to someone else—and her brats walk out of town. "I hope they're attacked by Indians," was his comment.

Simmons watched his wife trudge up the road. "Old lard-butted thing," he said, under his breath. "God, I hope I never see her again."

Like comments were being shared by all the men as they watched the women and kids move out.

Linda Potter and Lucille Stratton had elected to remain with their men. True to the end. Or 'til the money ran out—whichever came first.

Hunts-Long and his Flatheads were waiting by the creek. They had orders from Preacher to escort the

134

women to the flats and keep them there until the matter was settled in Bury—one way or the other.

"You can't know that for certain," Smoke said, looking at Audie, who had lowered his binoculars from the stream of humanity.

"With very little exception, my young friend. It doesn't hold true always, but water will seek its own level."

"We're gonna have to keep a sharp lookout for Richards's men, boy," Preacher said. "Them fifteen-eighteen riders he's got is all gunhands. Now you listen to me, boy," Preacher spun Smoke around to face him. "Them gold and silver mines that belong to them Big Three assayed out high. One mine, they got the gold assayed out at more than one hundred thousand dollars a ton. You know anything about gold, boy?"

Smoke shook his head.

"Two hundred dollars a ton is a workable mine, Smoke. So them boys ain't gonna just sit back and let you and us'ns destroy a fortune for 'em. We gonna have to be ready for nearabouts anything."

"I done warned them far'ners at the mines to stand clear of Bury," Matt said. "They took it to heart."

"How about the other miners?"

"Some of the miners here now was at the mining camp on the Uncompahgre," Preacher said. "The bettin' is high and fast."

"Who is the favorite?"

"Hell, boy," Preacher grinned. "Us'ns!"

17

According to the calendar, it was still the middle of spring in the mining country of East-Central Idaho. Someone should have told Mr. Summer that. By noon of the day of the pull-out, the temperature had soared and the sun was blisteringly hot. Bury, located in a valley, lay sullen and breezeless, the pocket in which it lay blocking the winds.

And the tempers of those trapped in the town were beginning to rival the thermometer.

One of Richards's men had discovered the blocked road and had hightailed back to the PSR ranch, informing Josh. Janey had just informed him as to Buck's real name. Josh Richards stood in the lushly appointed drawing room of the mansion and stared out at all the PSR holdings. Slowly, very slowly, a smile began playing at the corners of his mouth.

"What do you find so amusing, Josh?" Janey asked, watching the man.

"I will soon be the richest man in all of Idaho Territory," Josh replied. He carefully lit a cigar and inhaled slowly.

"I don't follow you."

"Think about it, Janey. We—you and I—are in the best possible position. Your brother is going to take some losses at Bury. He might even get himself killed. We can hope for that, at least." She shrugged. Whatever happened to Kirby didn't concern her at all. "All we have to do is pull the PSR men off the range, leaving only a skeleton crew with the herds, and station them around the house in armed circles. Let Smoke and his mountain men kill off as many as they can in Bury. For sure, Smoke will kill Stratton and Potter—that's what he came here to do. By the time the siege is over at Bury, Smoke's little army will be shot up and weakened; no way they could successfully attack this place. When they start to pull out, that's when I take my men and wipe them out." He grinned hugely. "Simple."

"So you're tossing Wiley and Keith to the wolves," she said matter-of-factly.

"Sure," he replied cheerfully. "Do you care?"

"Hell, no!" the woman said. "And there's something else, too."

"Oh?"

"You know the Army and the marshals will be in here investigating after it's over."

"Yeah. Sure. What about it?"

"Well, you just tell them some crap about Potter and Stratton. Tell them you found out about some illegal dealings they were involved in; you broke away from them. Tell the investigators you didn't want any part of anything illegal. You can even tell them you and your men joined up with Smoke and the mountain men in the assault on Bury. But," she said, holding up a warning finger, "that means that *everybody* has to die."

"You're a cold-blooded wench, Janey," he said with a great deal of pride and admiration.

"Just like you, love."

"Oh, I like it. I *like* it!" Josh began to pace the floor. He began to think aloud, talking as he paced. "I've got the best of the gunhands out here. Most of these men have been with me for years. They're loyal to me, and to me alone. They'll stand firm. I'll put all the newer men out on the range, looking after the cattle. Put the range-cook out there with them with ten days-two weeks of supplies and tell the boys to stay put." He grinned again, looking at Janey Jensen. "Love, we are going to *rule* Idaho Territory."

"I always wanted to be a queen," Janey said.

Josh and Janey began laughing.

To put a lid on the growing tempers in Bury, Stratton and Potter ordered free drinks at the town's many saloons and hurdy-gurdy houses. Then one drunk cowboy suggested they kick in the doors to the Pink House and have their way with the women barricaded inside.

About fifty men, in various stages of inebriation, marched up the main street and gathered in front of the Pink House. They began hooting and hollering and making all sorts of demands to the ladies. The hooting abruptly dipped into silence when the ladies inside shoved shotguns out through the barricaded windows. The sounds of hammers being jacked back was loud in the hot, still air.

The men took one look at a dozen double-barreled express guns pointing at them and calmed down.

"We are *closed!*" Miss Flora's voice came to the crowd. "You gentlemen have ten seconds to haul your ashes out of here. Aim at their privates, girls!"

A dozen shotguns were lowered, the muzzles aimed crotch-high.

The suddenly-sobered crowd hauled their ashes. Promptly.

Preacher watched it all through field glasses. He chuckled. He could not, of course, hear what was going on, but he could guess. "Them gals done read the scriptures to them ol' boys," he said. "I don't think the ladies is gonna be bothered no more after this."

One trapped PSR so-called gunhand emptied his pistol at the ridge overlooking the town. He stood in the center of the street and hurled curses at Smoke and the mountain men. Preacher reached for his Spencer and sighted the gunslick in. He emptied the tube, plowing up the ground around the man's boots. The cowboy shrieked in terror and dropped his pistol, running and falling and crawling for cover. He took refuge in the nearest saloon.

"We havin' fun now, Smoke," Preacher said, reloading. "But it's gonna turn ugly right soon."

"I know."

"You havin' second thoughts 'bout this, boy?"

"Not really. But if those men down there, with the exception of Potter and Stratton, wanted to leave, I wouldn't try to stop them."

"I's a-hopin you'd say that. Audie! Bring Smoke that there funny-lookin' thang you built."

Smoke took the megaphone and moved down the ridge, being careful not to expose himself. He lifted the megaphone to his lips.

"You men of Bury!" Smoke called. "Listen to me. It's Potter and Stratton and Richards I'm after. Not you. You don't owe him any loyalty. Any of you who wants to toss down his weapons and walk out can do so."

There was no reply of any kind from the town.

Smoke called, "I'm giving you people a chance to save your lives. The men you work for murdered my brother. They shot him in the back and left him to die."

"Rebel scum!" a voice called from the town.

Smoke shook his head. "The men you work for killed my pa."

139

"Big deal!" another voice shouted.

"Real nice folks down there," Audie muttered.

"The men you work for ordered out the men who raped and tortured and killed my wife, and killed my baby son," Smoke spoke through the megaphone.

Laughter from the town drifted up to Smoke and the mountain men. The laughter was ugly and taunting. "She probably wasn't nothin' but a whore anyways!" a voice shouted.

"I can't believe it," Smoke said, looking at Preacher. "I can't understand those types of people."

"I can," Audie said. "If you were my size, you would know just how cruel many people can be."

"Rider comin'," Tenneysee said.

Sam rode up and dismounted, walking to the edge of the ridge. He waited until Smoke and his friends climbed back up. "Givin' them folks a way out, Smoke?" he asked.

"I tried," Smoke replied.

"They ain't worth no pity," Sam said. "Lord knows I ought to know. I worked for them long enough. I seen them people do things that would chill you to the bone. I ain't never seen a bunch so hard-hearted as them people down there. Lie, steal, cheat, kill—them words don't mean nothing to them people. Simmons at the general store worked his momma to death. And I mean that. Then buried her in an unmarked grave. Cannon at the newspaper is so bad he's barred from the Pink House. Likes to beat women, if you know what I mean. And them ranchers out from town"—he spat on the ground—"hell, they just as bad. They run down and hanged a twelve-year-old boy when they found him leadin' off unbranded stock. He was just tryin' to feed his sick ma. It was pitiful. I seen some sights, but that one made me puke. Don't feel no sorrow for them folks down there, boys. They ain't

140

worth spit."

"Come and get us, gunhawk!" a voice yelled from the town. "We'll give you the same treatment the rest of your family got."

Smoke tossed the homemade megaphone to one side. "I tried," he said. "I tried."

The owners of the three other ranches located near Bury gathered at the home of Josh Richards. The owners had brought their so-called cowboys, many of whom were outlaws and gunfighters. Richards explained the situation at Bury—tactfully and pointedly leaving out that when his partners were dead, he would own it all.

"Well," Marshall of the Crooked Snake spread said, "I can see why we can't rush the town. Them mountain men would pick us off afore we got close enough to do any real damage."

The other two owners, Lansing of the Triangle and Brown of the Double Bar B, nodded their agreement. Lansing looked at Richards and asked, "You got a plan?"

"Not much of one. And my plan is rather self-serving, I'm afraid."

"Self what?" Marshall asked.

"It helps us but doesn't do much for those trapped in Bury," Richards explained.

"Hell with them!" Brown said. "We can always get more shopkeepers to come in."

No one mentioned Stratton or Potter. The men just looked at each other and smiled. Honor among thieves, and all that.

"Let's hear it," Lansing said.

"I don't understand it," Sam said. "Richards has about twenty gunhands out there at the ranch. And by

141

now he's called in Marshall and Lansing and Brown. Together, the four of them could put together forty-fifty men. That many men could put us in a box. I wonder what they're waiting for?"

Audie was thoughtful for a moment. "Perhaps this Richards person is hoping to gain from all this."

Smoke looked at him. "Sure. If Stratton and Potter get dead, Richards has it all."

"The loyalty of those men is overwhelming," Audie said drily.

"I wanted to burn down the town," Smoke admitted. "And I wanted revenge against those who killed my brother and pa, and who sent those men after me and my family. But as sorry as those people are down there in Bury, I don't want their blood on my hands."

Preacher seemed to breathe a sigh of relief. He knew the young man well, and knew Smoke did not want needless killing on his mind.

"Mayhaps you won't have to kill none of them down there," Preacher said.

"You chewin' 'round on something, Preacher," Beartooth said. "Spit 'er out."

"Well, lets us'ns slip word to Potter and Stratton that Richards is gonna lay out of this here fight. Kinda see what happens after that."

"An' juice it up a mite, too," Tenneysee said with a grin.

"Why, shore!" Preacher returned the grin. "Ain't nothing no better than a good joke." He thought about that for a moment. "At our age, that is."

18

Audie wrote out the first message to be delivered to the citizens of Bury. But it was so filled with big words nobody on the ridge knew what it said.

YOUR SO-CALLED CONFIDANTS HAVE ELECTED NOT TO CROSS THE RUBICON. THEY HAVE NOW SHOWN THEIR TRUE COLORS. THE MOMENT OF TRUTH IS NIGH. TO FIGHT US WOULD BE FOLLY. YOUR TRUE ADVERSARIES ARE YOUR ONE-TIME INTIMATES.

Tenneysee looked at the note and said, "I et Injun corn and sweet corn and flint corn, but I ain't never et no rubycorn. Whut the hell does food have to do with this here matter?"

"Imbecile!" Audie snapped at him. He opened his mouth to explain then closed it, knowing that if he tried to explain about the river it would only confuse matters further.

Audie stood and watched as Smoke laboriously printed another message, pausing often to lick the tip of the pencil stub.

Smoke tied the note to a stick, slipped down the ridge to within throwing distance, and tossed the message onto the main street.

Then Smoke, Sam, and the mountain men sat back and waited for the fun to begin.

Deputy Rogers had retrieved the stick. Since he couldn't read, he had no idea what was going on. He took the stick to Sheriff Reese. Reese read the message and took off at a run for Stratton and Potter.

"It's a trick!" Stratton said, his fat jowls quivering.

"I don't think so," Potter said. "You know perfectly well that by now all the ranchers know the road is blocked. There isn't a day goes by a dozen or more cowboys don't come into town to raise hell. Janey makes her grand appearance in town every day, weather permitting. No, I think we've been tossed to the lions. God*damn* Richards!"

"What are we gonna do?" Reese asked.

"I don't know. Give me time to think."

"If they try to send someone out of town, let them," Smoke said. Turning to Sam, he said, "And the one person they're going to meet will be you."

"I don't follow you," the puncher said.

"Your being fired was just a sham. A trick to get you on my side and see who I really was. You make them believe you're still working for Richards. Tell whoever they send out that Richards isn't going to interfere with me—he wants me to destroy the town, and everybody in it. Think you can pull that off?"

Sam grinned in the twilight. "You just watch me."

Sam rode out toward the north, reining up several miles from town. The mountain men built campfires to the south, the west, and the east of Bury. They deliberately left the north dark.

"That damned Jensen is so sure of himself he's not even guarding the north road," Reese said. He cursed under his breath.

"We got to be sure," Potter said. "Reese, send one of your men out to the ranch. Or as close to it as he can get. I've been thinking about something else, too." He looked at Reese. "Who gave the orders to fire Sam?"

"Richards said Mr. Stratton did."

"I never gave any such orders! You're sure Richards said it was my idea?" Stratton demanded.

"Well, yes, sir. But maybe he just used your name and forgot to tell you about it?"

"Why would he do that?"

"Because Sam worked for you, kinda."

But the seeds of suspicion had already been planted and were taking root. "Bull!" Stratton said.

"Looks bad, Keith," Potter said. "I'm beginning to think that just maybe Richards may have sent for Smoke."

"Yeah," his partner replied. "That would fit. That no good—" He bit back the profanity.

"Reese, you go snoop around town while your man is riding out. Go."

"Hold up!" Sam called from the darkness.

Deputy Rogers reined up and tried to peer through the gloom. "Sam? That you, Sam?"

"Yeah. Don't let none of them other riders catch you out here. They'll shoot you on sight."

"What other riders?" Rogers pulled in close to Sam.

"Crooked Snake, Triangle, Double Bar B—and any of Mr. Richards's gunhawks."

Rogers sighed. "Then it's true, Sam?"

"It's true." An idea began to form in Sam's head. He thought Smoke would like it. "I'm ridin' between town and the ranch, carryin' messages back and forth."

"Well, heck!" Rogers took off his hat and scratched his head. "I ain't got no messages to give you. Sorry."

"That's all right." You big dummy! Sam thought. "I got one for you to carry to Potter and Richards."

"They figured it out, Sam."

"Figured what out?"

"That you was all the time not fired and really workin' for Richards."

Sam breathed a bit easier. "I figured they would."

"And Mr. Richards sent for that there Smoke Jensen, didn't he?"

"I think so." This was gettin' better and better, Sam thought. But, he reminded himself, don't drop your guard. Rogers was big and stupid, but still a cold-blooded killer and cat quick.

"What's your message for them in town?"

Sam thought hard. "They're comin' in at noon, tomorrow."

"Well, then, I got a message for you. You tell 'em we'll be a-waitin'."

"No, we won't be waiting!" Stratton said.

"Huh?" Rogers was getting confused.

"Damn right!" Potter said.

"How we gonna get past Smoke and them mountain men?" Reese asked.

"Go holler up the hill," Stratton said. "Tell Smoke I wanna talk to him."

146

"What do you want?" Smoke called out of the high darkness.

"It was Richards that ordered your brother killed!" Potter yelled. "Me and Stratton didn't have nothing to do with it."

Smoke knew the man was lying. Knew it because of the dying confession of a TC hand a few years back. Smoke knew Potter had shot his brother. But since Sam had hightailed it back and told them all what he'd done, Smoke had agreed it was a fine idea. He'd play along.

"All right. I never knew who it was. But you was part of it," Smoke returned the darkness-shrouded shout.

"I won't deny that." Stratton's voice, "Neither of us. But what's done is done. I still have nightmares about it, though. If that makes any difference to you."

"That lyin' poke of buffalo chips!" Preacher said. "Only nightmares he ever has is someone stealin' his money."

"Yeah, I know," Smoke told his mentor. Raising his voice, he called, "What'd you want to talk to me about?"

"Ain't no call for us to be fightin' each other, Jensen. We know that Josh sent for you, probably payin' you good money, but whatever he's payin' you, we'll triple it. How about it? You're a hired gun. What difference does it make who pays you?"

"He's payin' me what's on that dodger. All in gold. You want to triple that, I'll take it in greenbacks or double eagles. Send MacGregor up here with the money. Let all the women leave the Pink House. Send them up here with Mac."

"And you'll do what?"

"I'll stand aside and let you three fight it out among you. Deal?"

"Who is Sam working for?" Potter called.

"Richards. But I know where he is, so I can get word to him."

"All right. It'll take us about an hour to get that much money together. We'll have to open the bank."

"I'll be here. In the meantime, you let those women go free. Deal?"

"It's a deal, Jensen."

"Sally?" Smoke called. "You hearin' all this?"

"Yes!" Sally's voice rose faintly from the edge of town.

"Then get some clothes and blankets together and come up here. You won't be harmed."

"We're on our way. And Mister Potter and Mister Stratton?" she yelled.

"We're right here, Miss Sally."

"We'll all be armed!"

No one could hear Stratton or Potter's muttered response. Probably just as well.

19

"Thank Sam for this," Smoke told Sally, as the women scampered up the hill and over the crest of the ridge. "He come up with this idea."

"Came up with," Sally corrected.

"Yes, ma'am," Smoke said.

"Lord have mercy!" Preacher muttered. "Rest of you boys look out now, 'cause them two gonna git to sparkin' and a-moonin' and a-carryin' on like who'd-a-thunk-it."

"Shut up, Preacher," Smoke told him.

"Most unrespectful young'un I ever hepped raise," Preacher said.

"*Dis*respectful," Sally corrected automatically.

"Lord, give this old man strength," Preacher mumbled, walking away.

About forty minutes after the women arrived, MacGregor called up the hill. "Do you actually expect one aging bookkeeper to behave as a pack animal and carry all this money up this mountain?"

"Comin' down," Smoke called.

"Any trouble?" Smoke asked, facing Mac on the hillside.

"Not a bit. Come on, let's walk." He tossed his suitcase to Sam and split the sacks of money between Smoke and himself. When they were out of normal earshot, Mac said, "I told Stratton and Potter I was no gunhand. I wanted out. They dismissed me without a second thought. Tell you the truth, I was relieved to get out. What in the world is going on, Mr. Jensen?"

"Let them destroy each other," Smoke said. "I'll clean up what's left."

"Very good thinking, young man. But what if one side or the other discovers your ruse?"

"My what?"

"Your trickery?"

"I'll worry about that if and when it happens."

"I think I would not like you for an enemy, young man," Mac said.

"When this is over, Mac, you'll probably never see me again. I intend to drop out of sight, change my name, hopefully get married, and settle down."

"I wish you luck, Kirby Jensen."

"Thank you, Mr. MacGregor."

With much good-natured grumbling among the mountain men, the ladies were settled in for the night. Guards were posted on the ridges, although none believed they were really necessary. The lights in the town of Bury blazed long into the night as the men prepared for war. Around midnight, very late for a western town, the lanterns and candles began to go out and the town was a dark shape in a velvet pocket.

The town was stirring before the first silver fingers of dawn began creeping over the mountains, touching the valleys and lighting the new day.

On the ridges, the men and women watched the citzens of Bury saddle horses and check out equipment.

"Mines is shut down tight," Dupre told Smoke.

The Frenchman had just completed a night-long tour of the country.

"The miners?"

"They around, but they keepin' their heads down and their butts outta sight. They know all hell's about to break loose around here."

"You see any PSR riders?"

"Several. They watchin' the town. Been there all night. I allow as to how they know 'bout the deal you made with Potter and Stratton. Seen one haul his ashes back towards the spread, hell bent for leather."

Smoke's grin was visible on the rim of the tin cup full of scalding black coffee. "Going to be a very interesting day," he said.

"So Wiley and Keith sold out to Smoke Jensen," Josh mused aloud. "Interesting. Thank you for that news." He waved the cowhand away and concentrated on his breakfast, conscious of the eyes on him as he ate.

Marshall and Lansing and Brown sat at the long table in the dining room. Marshall finally said, "They got us outnumbered just a tad."

"Not enough to cause us any concern," Josh replied. "As soon as they start pulling out, my riders will come fogging with the news and we'll have time to get ready. Besides, they're shopkeepers and store owners, not gunfighters."

Brown dashed cold water on that remark. "Josh, there ain't a man among them ain't a veteran of either the Civil War or a dozen Injun fights. They may be scoundrels and the like, but they ain't pilgrims."

Josh laid his knife and fork aside. He patted his mouth with a napkin. "Yes, you're right. They aren't going to just roll over and give up." He was thoughtful for a moment. He picked up a tiny silver bell and rattled it, bringing the houseman to the dining room. The other ranchers hid their amusement at that. "Thomas," Josh said to the black houseman, "tell Wilson and McNeil I wish to see them. Now!"

"Boss," Wilson said, uncomfortable in the lushly appointed dining room with carpet and heavy drapes and expensive chandelier. McNeil stood by his partner's side. The men held their hats in their hands.

"Pick a half-dozen boys from each ranch and take a dozen of our men. Ambush the men from town. To get to here, they've got to come through Levi Pass. Hit them there. Draw enough ammo and food for several days in the field. And, Wilson . . ." He met the man's eyes. "If you fail, don't bother coming back."

"Yes, sir."

Smoke stood on the ridge overlooking the now-deserted town of Bury. His eyes were bleak. Savage-looking. Sally stood by his side, gazing up at him.

"What are you thinking, Smoke?" she asked.

"Take a good look at Bury, Sally."

"I see it. What about it?"

" 'Cause this is the last time you'll be able to see it."

"Are we pulling out?"

"No. Not yet."

"Then . . . ?"

"I'm going to burn it to the ground." He checked both his Colts and picked up his Henry repeating rifle. He slowly walked down the hill, Matt, Preacher, Tenneysee, and Greybull following him.

Sally stood on the crest of the ridge, Audie by her side—standing on a large rock. Little Ben joined them, rubbing sleep from his eyes.

"What are your feelings toward and for that young man?" Audie asked.

"I love him," Sally said quietly.

"It bloomed very quickly between you two. Are you certain of your feelings?"

"Yes."

"When this is over," Audie said, "I believe the burning hate within him will vanish. It's been an all-consuming thing with him for a long time. But hear me out, young woman. No matter where you two go . . ."

"Three," Sally said, putting her arm around Ben's shoulders.

Audie smiled. "No matter where the *three* of you go, Smoke's reputation will follow. No matter how hard he tries, he will never be able to completely shake it. This is wild and savage country, and it will be so for many years to come. If you settle somewhere to ranch, there will be outlaws who will try to take what is yours, and Smoke will stand up to them. Word will get around, and tinhorns and would-be gunhands will follow, the only thing in their minds being the desire to be the man who killed the fastest gun in the west. Then you will have to leave and settle elsewhere, for Smoke is not the type of man to back down. He desperately wants to settle down, live a so-called normal life, but it is going to be extremely difficult. You're going to have to be very strong."

"Yes," Sally said, not taking her eyes from her young man. And she knew he was hers. "I am aware of that. Mr. Audie . . ."

"Just Audie. My last name is no longer important."

"Audie. I am a woman of some means. I recently came into quite a large sum of money. Perhaps Smoke will consent to go back east and live."

Audie smiled. "What would he do, Sally? Can you imagine him in some office, with a tie and starched collar?"

She laughed softly. She could not imagine that.

"He is a man of the west, of the frontier. This is his land. He would not be happy anywhere else."

And I would not be happy anywhere without him, she thought. Odd that I have known him for so brief a time and yet am so certain of my feelings. But I am certain.

Only a few people remained in town, and those looked very suspiciously at Smoke and the mountain men. Their suspicion soon turned to hard reality.

"Pack up and clear out," Smoke informed them. "Get your gear together, and move out!"

"You can't just come in here and force us out!" a man protested.

Smoke looked at the man, open contempt in his eyes. "You did what before you came here?"

The man shuffled his feet and refused to reply. He dropped his eyes.

Smoke looked at the small group left behind in the town. "You all knew you were working for crud and crap. And you didn't care. All you cared about was money. And it didn't make a damn to any of you where that money came from, or how you earned it. I have no sympathy for any of you. Get your gear together and get out of here."

They got.

"Round up all the pack animals you can find," Smoke asked the mountain men. He waved all but four of the men down from the ridge, leaving those as guards. "We're gonna give some of these homesteaders in this area a second chance. Food, clothes, boots,

154

guns, equipment. We'll pass it out later. Let's get to work."

What couldn't be packed out on horses and mules was passed up the hill like a bucket brigade. Soon the stores were emptied. The town was strangely silent and ghostlike. Audie summed it up.

"This town had no heart," the little man said. "One cannot feel sorry for destroying something that never lived."

Smoke tossed the first torch into a building. The dry wood was soon blazing, spreading to the adjoining building. Black greasy smoke began pouring into the sky in spiraling waves. The dry pine began popping like sixguns. Soon the heat was so intense it forced the men back to the coolness of the ridge.

"Soon as them people see this smoke, they'll get the message," Preacher said.

"Those that are left alive," Smoke said softly.

20

Levi Pass lay sullen under the heat of the sun. Bodies littered the pass; men and animals sprawled in soon-to-be bloated death. The first contingent of men, led by Deputy Payton, had been knocked from their saddles in a hard burst of rifle fire from the rocks above the pass. Among the first to die were Rosten, the stable manager; Simmons, who ran the general store; and Deputy Payton. A sheriff back in Iowa would never learn that he could destroy the murder warrant he held for Payton.

Among the gunhands in the rocks, McNeil and a rider from the Crooked Snake and Triangle lay dead. The moaning of the wounded, on both sides, softly drifted out of and above the dust and gunsmoke of the pass.

Then the men saw the smoke belching into the skies.

"What the hell?" Wilson muttered from behind his shoulder on the ridge.

"That bastard Jensen has torched the town!" Potter said.

"Oh, my God!" Stratton said, his face dusty and his elegant clothing torn and dirty. "All our records."

Wilson laughed. "Looks like your boy done turned on you!" he called down into the pass.

"Our boy!" Potter yelled. "He started out workin' for you."

"You lie!" Wilson yelled. "You brung him in!"

"What the hell are you talking about?" Stratton screamed.

Wilson's long-unused gray cells began working. "Now wait just a minute," he called. "You tryin' to claim you didn't hire Jensen?"

"Sure we did," Potter yelled. "But we hired him away from Richards. Last night. Richards brought him in to kill us."

"You're crazy!" Wilson yelled. "Just hold on a second. Everybody stop shootin'. We got to talk about this."

"I don't trust you!" Potter screamed. "You're up to something."

"I ain't up to nothin', you fat hog!" Wilson yelled. "You and Stratton was the ones who wanted it all. Ya'll caused all this trouble."

Wilson stood up from behind the boulder.

Sheriff Reese lifted his rifle and shot the man in the stomach. The .44 round knocked the gunhand backward. He died with a scream on his bloody tongue.

A Crooked Snake rider shot Cannon, the newspaper editor, in the center of his forehead. Cannon was dead before he hit the rocky ground of the pass road.

Levi Pass erupted and rocked with pistol and rifle fire. Britt, a rider for the Crooked Snake, crouched behind his cover and mulled matters over in his mind. He was getting the feeling that that damned Smoke Jensen had set them all up; made fools out of everybody; sitting back and laughing while they was shooting at each other.

He slipped from his cover and inched his way toward the timber, where the horses were tied. He spurred his mount, heading for the PSR spread. He wanted to tell his boss what he'd just heard.

Behind him, the savage gunfight continued, the air filled with shouts and curses and the screaming of the wounded and the silence of the dead.

"Now wait a minute!" Josh said. "Tell me again what you heard back at the pass."

Britt repeated what he'd heard between Wilson, Stratton, and Potter.

Lansing went to a window of the mansion and looked toward the town. Though miles away, he could clearly see the black smoke pouring into the sky. "Shore nuff on fire," he said.

"He played us against each other," Richards said. "And I played right into his hands. He set me up like a kid with a string toy. That damn gunhawk *knew* what I'd do." He sat down heavily. "I don't like being made a fool of. I don't like it worth a damn!"

"He shore done 'er though," Marshall rubbed it in a bit. Marshall and the other ranchers were every bit as tough as Richards, with no back-up in them. They were all thieves and murderers, their pasts as black as midnight.

Richards's gaze was bleak. "Gather up the men. We're ridin'."

"Richards is anything but a fool, Smoke," Sally told him. Standing beside her, Sam solemnly nodded his head. "If he puts all this together, then you've lost your element of surprise."

"I don't think either side wiped the other out in that pass," Preacher opined. "And we ain't heared no gunfire in more'un an hour. I think they got to talkin' and figured things out."

Smoke looked at Tenneysee. "The supplies hidden?"

"B'ar couldn't find 'em."

"We'll get the women over to Becky's place and leave them there. We'll head for the timber and make them come after us."

"The ranches lay in a half circle around Bury," Sam said. "Marshall, Lansing, and Brown will have most of their men out looking for you; only a handful will be at the ranches. The real cowhands and punchers will be with the herds. They're cowboys, not gunslicks."

"Then we'll leave them be," Smoke said. "When we get ready to scatter the herds, we'll tell the punchers to take off for new ground."

"They'll go," Sam said.

"Let's ride."

Leaving what was once the Idaho Territory town of Bury still smoking and burning behind them, the outnumbered band of ancient mountain men, gunhands, and ladies saddled up and drifted into the deep timber, with Sam leading the way. At Becky's small farm, Sam explained the situation to Becky and she agreed to help any way she could. Little Dan introduced the kids to the mountain men. Becky's kids had seen a lot during their time in the west, but absolutely nothing compared with the sight of the old mountain men, all dressed in buckskins and colorful sashes and armed to the teeth. And they certainly had never seen anything to match Audie. No taller than the children, the tiny mountain man captivated the kids. When he jumped up on a stump and began telling fairy tales, the kids sat around him listening, spellbound.

Sally and Smoke walked a short distance from the cabin. "Do we talk now, Smoke?" she asked.

"I reckon so." He waited for her to correct his grammar. She did not.

"Very well. I want to see the west, Smoke. And I want you to show it to me."

"Dangerous, Sally. And not very ladylike. You'd have to ride astride."

She hid her smile. Her father had paddled her behind several times as a child for doing just that. "I'm sure I could cope."

Buck let that alone. "What is it you want to see?"

"The high lonesome," she said without hesitation.

"It's all around you here."

"You know what I mean, Smoke. The real high lonesome. The one you and the other mountain men talk about. When you speak of that, your voice becomes soft and your eyes hold a certain light. That's the high lonesome I would like to see."

"You'll have to learn to shoot," Smoke said dubiously.

"Then I shall."

"Camp and live out in the wilderness."

"All right."

"It won't be easy. Your skin will be tanned and your hands will become hard with callouses."

"I expect that."

Smoke kept his face noncommittal. He had hoped Sally would want to see his world; the world that he knew was slowly vanishing. There would be time.

He hoped.

"All right," he said.

She rose up on her tiptoes and kissed him on the cheek. "You come back to me," she said.

He did not reply. That was something he could not guarantee.

* * *

"Nothing left, Boss," Long reported back to Josh Richards. "Jensen burned the whole place to the ground."

Potter and Stratton were now once more joined with Richards. The opposing sides had ceased fighting in Levi Pass and begun talking. The men were chatting amicably when Richards, Marshall, Lansing, and Brown rode up with their men.

"Nothing?" Burton asked. "My apothecary shop is gone?"

"There ain't nothing left," Long said. "And Jensen and them old bastards is gone. Took the women and left. I cut their sign but lost it in the rocks."

"Sam?" Richards asked.

"No sign of him."

"That was a nice hotel," Morgan said wistfully.

"Beautiful church," Necker said. "Takes a heathen to destroy a house of God."

Simpson spat on the ground. "You damned fake!" he told Necker. "You ain't no more no preacher than I is. I knowed all along I'd seen you 'fore. Now I remember. I knowed you up in Montana Territory. Elkhorn. You was dealing stud and pimpin'. You kilt Jack Harris when he caught you cold-deckin' him."

"You must be mistaken, my good man," Necker said. But his face was flushed. "I came from—"

"Shut up, Necker. Or whatever your name is," Lansing said. "Now I'm gonna tell you all something Or remind you of it. Remind you all of a lot of things. They ain't none of us clean. We all—*all of us*—got dodgers out on us. Now we can't none of us afford to lose this fight. 'Cause you all know damn well when that stage reports the town is burnt, the Army's gonna come in here and start askin' a bucket full of questions. That means all them pig farmers and nesters in this area's gotta go in the ground. Cain't none of 'em

161

be allowed to live and flap their gums." He glared at Richards. "I tole you time after time that I didn't trust that there Scotsman. He ain't what he appears to be. Bet on it. When the trouble started, he shore wanted to leave in a hurry, didn't he?"

"Yes, he did," Stratton said. "And it appeared that he and Smoke Jensen were friends."

"They got to die," Marshall said. "All of them."

"What about them farmers' kids?" a gunhand asked.

"Them, too," Brown said. "Cain't nobody be left alive to point no finger at us."

"I want Smoke Jensen!" Dickerson gasped from his blankets on the ground. Still gravely wounded, the outlaw had insisted upon coming to the pass rather than leaving with the men Smoke had ordered out before burning the town.

The men ignored him. Dickerson's wounds had reopened, and all those present knew the outlaw and murderer was not long for this world.

"Ya'll hear me?" Dickerson said.

"Aw, shut up and die!" Necker told him. "We're busy."

Dickerson fell back on his dirty blankets and died.

Smoke, Sam, and the mountain men rode west, toward Marshall's Crooked Snake spread. The Frenchman, Dupre, was ranging ahead of the main body of men. About two miles from the ranch, Smoke pulled up, waiting for Dupre to return with a scouting report.

During this quiet, which, all knew, would soon become very rare, Preacher talked with Smoke. "You beginnin' to feel all the hate leave your craw, boy?"

"Yes," Smoke admitted.

"That's good. That's a mighty fine little gal back yonder at that nester place."

"She wants to see the high lonesome."

"Be tough on a woman. You gonna show her?"

Smoke hesitated. "Yes."

Preacher spat a stream of brown tobacco juice on the ground, drowning a bug. "Soon as this here affair is done, you two best git goin'. High lonesome will soon be gone. Civil-lie-say-shon done be takin' over, pilgrims ruinin' everything. Be a fine thing to show that woman, though. She's tough, got lots of spunk. She'll stand by you, I's thinkin'."

"Us, you mean, don't you?"

"You mean the boy?"

Smoke shook his head. "I mean Sally, Little Ben, me, and you."

"No, Smoke," Preacher said. "I'll be leavin' with my pards. They's still some corners of this land that's high and lonesome. No nesters with their gawd-damned barbed wire and pigs and plows. Me and Tenneysee and Audie and Nighthawk and all the rest—wal, our time's done past us, boy. Mayhaps you'll see me agin—mayhaps not. But when my time is nigh, I'll be headin' back to that little valley where you hammered my name in that stone. There, I'll jist lay me down and look at the elephant. I'll warn you now, son. This will be the last ride for Deadlead and Matt. They done tole me that. They real sick. Got that disease that eats from the inside out."

"Cancer?"

"That'd be it, I reckon. They gonna go out with the reins in they teeth and they fists full of smokin' iron. They'll know when it's time. You a gunhand, boy; you understand why they want it thataway, don't you?"

"Yes."

163

"All right. It's all said then. When it's time for me and the boys to leave, I don't want no blubberin', you understand?"

"Have you ever seen me blubber?"

"Damn close to it."

"You tell lies, old man."

Preacher's eyes twinkled. "Mayhaps one or two, from time to time."

"Here comes Dupre."

"We gonna be runnin' and ridin' hard for the next two-three days, son. We'll speak no more of this. When this is over, me and boys will just fade out. 'Member all I taught you, and you treat that there woman right. You hear?"

"I hear."

"Let's go bring this to an end, boy."

21

"If you're cowboys, turn those ponies' noses west and ride out. If you're gunhands, make your play," Smoke said.

The three riders on the Crooked Snake range slowly turned their horses, being very careful to keep their hands away from sixguns. They sat and stared at the mountain men and at Smoke.

"We're drawin' thirty a month and found," one said. "That ain't exactly fightin' pay."

"You got anything back at the bunkhouse worth dyin' over?"

"Not a thing."

"You boys ride out. If you've a mind to, come back in three-four days. They'll be a lot of cattle wandering around with no owners. You might want to start up some small spreads in this area."

"You be the outlaw, Smoke Jensen?" a cowboy asked.

"I'm Jensen. But I'm no outlaw."

"Mister, if you say you're an African go-riller, you ain't gonna git no argument from me," another cowboy said.

"Fine. You boys head on toward the Salmon. Drift back in three-four days. We'll be gone, and so will the ranches. The homesteaders will still be here, though. Unless you want to see me again, leave them be. Understand?"

"Mr. Jensen, I'll even help 'em *plow*!"

Smoke smiled. "Take off."

The punchers took off.

"Five, maybe six gunnies at the ranch," Beartooth said, riding up.

Smoke looked at Powder Pete. "Got some dynamite with you?"

"You don't have to say no more." Powder Pete wheeled his mustang and took off for the ranch, Smoke and Sam and the mountain men hard after him.

"How do you boys want it?" Smoke called to the deserted-appearing ranch.

A rifle shot was the only reply.

"Hold your fire," Smoke told his people. Raising his voice, he shouted, "Your boss payin' you so much money you'd die for him?"

"Hell with you, Jensen!" the shout drifted to Smoke. "Come git us if you got the sand to do it."

Smoke looked at Powder Pete. "Blow 'em out!"

The old mountain man grinned and slipped silently away. About five minutes later, the bunkhouse exploded, the roof blowing off. A dynamite charge blew the porch off the main house, collapsing one side of the house. Smoke and the mountain men poured a full minute of lead into the house.

"I'm done with it!" a man shouted from the dynamite-ruined and bullet-pocked house. "Lemme ride out and I'm gone."

"Take what's on your back and clear out!" Smoke yelled. "How 'bout you other men?"

"There ain't no other men," the man shouted, a bitter edge to his voice. "Two was in the bunkhouse. Rafter got another in here. Lead took the others. I'm it!"

"Clear out and don't come back."

"You just watch my dust, Jensen."

They watched it fade out, the gunhand riding toward the west. He did not look back.

"Check the house for wounded, then burn it all," Smoke said.

"You got a mean streak in you," Preacher said. "Shore didn't git it from me."

Smoke grinned at the man who had helped raise him. Preacher was as mean and vindictive as a wounded grizzly.

"I allow as to how we ain't gonna bury them gunhawks in the house," Preacher said, not putting it in question form.

"Somewhere, sometime, they had a ma," Smoke said. "She'd wanna know her boy was buried proper."

"I'd afraid you say that," Preacher bitched. "I ain't never found no shovel to fit my hand."

"There goes my ranch," Marshall said, looking west into the sky. There was no bitterness in his voice, only a grudging admiration.

The hundred-odd men sat their saddles and stared at the black smoke pluming into the sky.

"We can still save the cattle," one of his men said.

"You want them, you save them," Marshall replied. "I'm headin' out."

"Where the hell you think you goin'?" Lansing asked.

"I'm pullin' out. You boys got any smarts, you'll do the same. I just realized that we ain't gonna stop this Jensen. If'n a man's right, and he jist keeps on comin', ain't nothing or nobody gonna stop him. And you know what, boys? Jensen's right."

"*Right?*" Potter squalled. "He comes in here and ruins everything we worked to build and you sit there and say the man's right?"

Marshall chuckled grimly. "That's it, boys. Everything we got we built on stole money and the blood of others. Hell with it. I'm pullin' out." He wheeled his horse and turned his back to the others.

Josh Richards jerked up his rifle and shot the man in the back. Marshall fell from the saddle, his spine severed. He lay on the ground, looking at the men through pain-filled eyes. "Should have known one of you would do that," he gasped.

Stratton shot the man between the eyes.

Potter looked at what remained of Marshall's men. "Stay with us. All his cattle, his mine holdings—everything is yours if we win this fight."

"We'll stay," one hard-faced Crooked Snake gunnie said. "I never liked Marshall no how."

"Let's ride."

"What do we do with the cattle?" Audie asked.

"Leave them for those cowboys," Smoke said. "They seemed like pretty decent boys to me."

"The cattle on Richards's place?" Tenneysee asked.

"That's another story. We'll give them to the nesters and the miners."

"Seems fair enough," Lobo said. "I damned shore don't want 'um."

"Someone has to meet the stage and turn it around," Smoke said. "Any volunteers?"

"MacGregor said he'd do it," Sam spoke. "But I don't like the idee of one man waitin' out there all alone with a hundred or so gunhands on the prowl."

"You go back and meet the stage with him," Audie suggested. "I should imagine you and your ladyfriend will be settling in this area. So the less you have to do with this matter, the better. Agreed, Smoke?"

"Good idea. Take off, Sam. I'll see you when this is over."

Reluctantly, Sam agreed and rode out, back to Becky's cabin.

"Lansing's Triangle is almost due north from here," Matt said. "We hit there next?"

"That's what they would expect us to do, isn't it?" Smoke asked, a hard grin on his lips.

"Oh, you sneaky, boy!" Preacher said. "You as sneaky as a rattler."

"Whut you two jawin' about?" Phew asked.

"We head straight east," Smoke explained. "For Brown's Double Bar B. I'm betting Richards and all the rest are hightailing right now to set up an ambush around Lansing's spread."

"At's rat good thankin', boy," Beartooth said. "I can tell Preacher hepped raise you."

Preacher stuck out his skinny chest. "Done a damn good job of 'er, too."

"Don't start braggin'," Greybull said. "I been listenin' to you bump them gums of yourn for fifty years. Sickenin'."

"Hush up, you mule-ridin' giant!" Preacher told him.

The other mountain men joined in.

They were still grousing and bitching and hurling insults at one another as they rode off.

"We're spread thin," Brown said to Richards. "Real thin."

"But when they come," Stratton said, "we'll have them in a circle. All we have to do is close up the bottom of the pinchers and trap them."

"*If* they come," Lansing said. "I don't trust that damned Jensen. He's a devil."

"He's just a man," Sheriff Reese said sourly.

"A hell of a man," Richards said. "Janey's brother."

"What!" Potter shouted.

"Janey told me before I left the ranch. She knew all along that she'd seen him somewhere, but she didn't put it together until a few days ago."

"What'd she say do with him?" Stratton asked.

Richards shrugged. "Kill him."

Dawn broke hot and red over the valley that Brown called his Double Bar B spread. During the night, Dupre and Deadlead had slipped into the ranch area and found it deserted except for the cook. They had put him on the road after he told them that all the men drawing fighting pay were out with the boss. Just punchers riding herd on the cattle. Give them a chance, and they'd haul their ashes quick.

That was what Smoke was now doing. Alone.

The punchers looked up as the midnight-black stallion with the tall rider approached their meager camp. They all knew, without being told, who they were facing.

"We're cowboys, not gunhawks," one puncher said. "We ain't lookin' for no trouble."

"Then you won't have any," Smoke told him. "Get your gear, pack it up, and ride out.' He made them the same offer he had made the Crooked Snake cowboys.

"Sounds good to me," a puncher said. "We gone, Mister Jensen."

Smoke watched them ride out, leaving the herd without a backward glance.

He waved the mountain men in. Lobo inspected the main house.

"Place is a damned pigsty," he reported back.

"Well, let's roast some pigs," Smoke said.

"That son of a bitch!" Brown shouted, jumping up, his eyes to the east. "He's fired my ranch."

Richards looked at the smoke pouring into the sky. There was a look of grudging admiration on the man's cruel face.

"I've had it!" Morgan said. "Me and Burton and Hallen and some of the others been talkin'. We're pullin' out, headin' west."

The others looked at the rifles in the mens' hands. Potter stepped in before gunfire could start.

"All right!" he shouted. "How many of you are leaving?"

Nearly all the men from town were leaving, with the exception of Sheriff Reese and his so-called deputies.

"I gather you're going to join your families?" Richards said with a smile on his face.

"That's crap!" Reverend Necker said. "I don't care if I ever see that old bat again."

"Don't any of you ever set a boot in this part of the country again," Stratton warned.

"Don't you worry," Burton said.

The townspeople rode out without looking back.

Looking around them, the ranchers and gunhands could see where others had deserted them during the night. Quietly slipped away into the darkness. What remained were the hardcases.

"They wasn't much help anyways," a gunnie from the Crooked Snake said. "I never did trust none of them."

"Rider comin' hard," another gunslick said, looking toward the southeast.

Simpson reined up, his horse blowing hard. "Min-

171

ers quit!" he said. "All of 'em. Said they ain't workin' for none of you no more."

Stratton started cursing. Potter and Richards let him curse until he ran down.

"Where's all them townies goin'?" Simpson asked.

"Turned yeller and run," Long told him.

"Let 'em go. They's only in the way." He looked at Richards. "That smoke back yonderways—that the Double Bar B?"

"Yeah." He twisted in the saddle, the leather creaking. He looked at the men gathered around him. "Any the rest of you boys want to turn tail and run?"

That question was met by silence and hard eyes.

"We gonna make them mountain men and Mister Jensen come to us," Richards declared. "Where's the nearest nester spread from here?" He tossed the question to anyone.

" 'Bout ten miles," a gunslick said. "Next one is about four miles from that one."

"Dent," Richards looked at a mean-eyed rider. "Take a couple of boys and go burn them out. Black, you take a couple men and burn out the next pig farmer's family. That ought to bring Mister High-And-Mighty Jensen on the run." Richards started laughing. "And while you're doing that, the rest of us will be setting up an ambush."

"What about the wimmin and kids?" a gunhawk named Cross asked.

"What about them?" Potter asked.

"I thought we agree on that?" Stratton said.

"They have to die," Richards said. "All of them."

22

The homesteader's cabin appeared deserted when Dent and the others galloped into the front yard, the horses' hooves trampling over a flower bed and a newly planted garden. Normally, that action alone would bring the wife on a run, squalling and flapping her apron. It was a game the punchers liked to play with nesters, for few cowboys liked nesters, with their gardens and fences.

This time their destructive actions were met with silence.

Inside the cabin, the man lifted a finger to his lips, telling his wife and kids to be still. The wife nodded and moved to a gun slit in the logs, a .30–30 in her hands. Her husband held a double-barreled shotgun, the express gun loaded with buckshot. That painted lady from town had ridden by the day before, warning them to be on guard. All them ladies from the Pink House was riding around, warning the other homesteaders what was happening. First time he'd ever met a . . . a . . . one of them ladies. Nice looking woman.

He eased the hammers back on the shotgun.

"Set the damned place on fire!" Dent yelled. "Burn 'em out."

Those were the last words Dent would speak in his life. The homesteader's shotgun roared, the buckshot from both barrels catching Dent in the chest and face. The charge lifted the gunhand from the saddle, tearing off most of his face and flinging him several yards away from his horse.

The homesteader's wife shot the second rider in the chest with her .30–30 just as the oldest boy fired from the hog pen. Three riderless horses stood in the front yard.

The homesteader and his family moved cautiously out of hiding. "Take their guns and stable their horses," the man said. "Mother, you get the Bible. Son, you get a couple shovels. We'll give them a Christian burial."

Black lifted himself up to one elbow. The pain in his chest was fierce. He coughed up blood, pink and frothy. Lung-shot, he thought.

Black looked around him. Douglas and Cross were lying in the front yard of the pig farmer's cabin. They looked dead. *Hell*, they were dead!

Who'd have thought it of a damned nester?

Black looked up at the damned homesteader in those stupid-looking overalls. Man had a Colt in each hand. Damn sure knew how to use them, too.

"Never thought a stinkin' pig farmer would be the one to do me in," Black gasped the words.

"I was a captain in the War Between the States," the man spoke calmly. "First Alabama Cavalry."

"Well, I'll just be damned!" Black said.

"Yes," the farmer agreed. "You probably will."

Black closed his eyes and died.

"No smoke," Lansing observed.

"Thought I heard gunfire, though," Potter said.

"Yeah," Stratton said. "But who is shootin' who?"

Richards's stomach felt sour, like he'd drank a glass of clabbered milk. Sour. Yeah, that was the word for it. Sour. Whole damned business was going sour. And all because of one man. He looked around him.

174

Something was out of whack. Then it came to him. About ten or so men were gone, had slipped quietly away. Hell with them. They still had fifty-sixty hard-cases. More than enough to do the job.

Or was it?

He shook that thought away. Can't even think about that. He wondered what that damned Smoke was doing right now.

Janey had never seen a more disreputable-looking bunch of men in all her life. *God!* they looked older than death.

Except for her brother.

Janey looked at the dead gunhands lying in the front yard. The gunhands Josh had left behind to protect her. That was a joke. But there wasn't anything funny about it.

"Hello, brother," she said.

"Sis," Smoke returned the greeting.

"Well, now what?" Her voice was sharp.

"How much money you have in the house, sis?"

"You going to rob me?"

"No."

She shrugged. "Quite a bit, I guess, brother. Yeah. Lots of money in the house."

"Can you ride astride?"

"Kid," she laughed, "I've ridden more things astride than I care to think about."

Smoke knew what his sister meant. He ignored it. "Change your clothes, get what money you can carry, and clear out. I don't care where you go, just go. I don't ever want to see you again."

Her laugh was bitter. "You always could screw up every plan I ever made."

"Don't you care what Richards did to your pa and

brother?" he asked.

"Hell, no!"

He remembered his pa's letter. "I guess Pa was right, Janey. He said you were trash."

"Rich trash, baby brother. Doesn't that bother you?"

"Money rich, sis. That's all."

"And you don't think that's sufficient?"

"If you do, I feel sorry for you."

"Then that makes you a fool, Kirby!"

He shrugged. "One hour, Janey. That's all the time I'm giving you. Pack up and clear out."

She nodded and turned her back to him. She stopped and turned around. She gave him an obscene gesture, spat on the porch, and walked into the house.

"You rat sure there wasn't some mixup in babies when she were birthed?" Preacher asked. "You sure she's your sis?"

"I'm sure."

Janey left riding like a man and holding the rope of the pack animal.

"Aren't you the least bit worried about your man?" Smoke had asked her.

"Shoot the son of a bitch as far as I'm concerned," had been her reply. She had spurred her horse and ridden off without looking back.

"What a delightful young woman," Audie said, the crust about an inch thick in his voice.

Smoke watched his only living relative—that he knew of—ride away. He knew he should feel something—but he didn't.

Yes, he did, he corrected.

Relief in the fact that he had found her alive and had offered her a chance to live and she had taken it.

He shook his head.

So he still felt something for her.

But damn little.

"Burn the house to the ground," he said. He looked around him. Deadlead and Matt were gone. His eyes met Preacher's gaze.

"They gone to buy us some time," the mountain man said. "They won't be back."

Smoke nodded his head.

"I tole 'em not to kill Stratton, Potter, or Richards," Preacher said. "You wanted them yourself."

"I do. Thanks."

"Think nuttin' of it. I give 'em to you fer your birthday. Rest of us be takin' off shortly. You know what I mean."

Smoke knew.

Two riders left their saddles before the sounds of the rifle fire reached the column of outlaws. The two men were dead before they hit the ground.

"What the hell?" Reese yelled.

"Ambush!" Stratton screamed.

Two more men were flung backward and to the ground, dead and dying.

"There they are!" Rogers hollered, pointing to a ridge. "Come on, let's get 'em!"

A dozen riders looked at each other, nodded minutely, and slowly wheeled their horses, riding in the opposite direction.

"Come back here, you cowards!" Potter screamed.

"Let them go," Richards said calmly. "Nobody fire at them."

His partners looked at him strangely.

"It's over," Richards said. "We're walking-around dead men and don't even know it."

"What do you mean?" Stratton's scream was tinted with hysteria.

"Look," Richards said, pointing toward his ranch house.

A huge cloud of black smoke was filling the air.

"The PSR house!" Reese yelled.

"Yeah," Richards said. He smiled. "And you can bet my darling Janey has taken all the cash in the house—which was considerable; she'd need a pack animal to carry it off—and is gone. Her brother wouldn't kill her."

"Well, you're taking it damned calm," Potter said.

"No reason to get upset. What is done is done."

One of the dying gunhawks on the ground moaned.

"Hosses comin' at us," a gunnie said. "Holy crap!" he yelled. "We're being charged!"

Deadlead and Matt were in the middle of the riders before the gunhands could really believe it was all taking place. With the reins in their teeth and their fists wrapped about the butts of .44s and .45s, the old mountain men emptied their pistols and had shucked their rifles before anyone else could fire a shot. Richards had trotted his horse off a few hundred yards and was sitting quietly, watching it all, Potter and Stratton with him. Stratton's face was ashen, his hands trembled, his once fine clothes were torn and dirty.

Eight more riders had joined the four on the ground before the mountain men were blasted from their saddles. Matt rose to his boots, roaring as his blood poured from his wounds.

"Somebody kill that damned nigger!" a gunslick yelled.

Matt shot the man between the eyes with a pistol he'd grabbed from off the ground.

Deadlead jerked a gunhawk off his horse and snapped his neck as easily as wringing the neck of a chicken.

Twenty guns roared. The riddled bodies of the mountain men fell to the already-blood-soaked dust.

Deadlead lifted his bloody head and looked at Sheriff Dan Reese. "Thank you, boys." He fell to the ground, dead, beside his lifelong friend.

"He *thanked* me!" Reese said, horror in his voice. "Thanked me? For *what*?" he screamed.

"If you don't understand," Richards said, "there is no point in my trying to explain it to you." He looked around him. "Long! Take a couple of boys. Get over to that woman's cabin Sam is sweet on. Kill her and them snot-nosed brats."

"With pleasure," the short, stocky gunhand said with a grin. "I just might get me a taste of that gal 'fore I do."

"Your option," Richards said.

Long took Deputy Weathers and rode toward the nester cabin. They were, despite all that had happened, in high spirits. Becky was a one fine-lookin' piece of woman. They rode arrogantly into the front yard, scattering chickens and tramping the flower garden.

"You in the house!" Long called. "Get your tail out here, woman."

The door opened and Nighthawk stepped out, his big hands wrapped around .44s. He blew Long and Weathers clean out of their saddles. He tied the dead men to the saddles and slapped the horses on the rump, sending them home.

"Those two won't bother me again," Becky said.

"Ummm," Nighthawk replied.

23

The ever-shrinking band of outlaws and gunhands looked toward the west. Another cloud of black smoke filled the air.

Lansing began cursing. "How in the hell are them old men doin' it?" he yelled. "We're fightin' a damned bunch of ghosts."

"Are you stayin' or leavin'?" Stratton asked.

"Might as well see it through," the man said bitterly. Those were the last words he would speak on this earth. A Sharps barked, the big slug taking the rancher in the center of his chest, knocking him spinning from his saddle.

"I've had it!" a gunhand said. He spun his horse and rode away. A dozen followed him. No one tried to stop them.

"Look all around us," Brown said.

The men looked. A mile away, in a semicircle, ten mountain men sat their ponies. As if on signal, the old mountain men lifted their rifles high above their heads.

Turkel, one of the most feared gunhawks in the territory, looked the situation over through field glasses. "That there's Preacher," he said, pointing. "That'un over yonder is the Frenchman, Dupre. That one ridin' a mule is Greybull. That little bitty shithead is the midget, Audie. Boys, I don't want no truck with them old men. I'm tellin' you all flat-out."

The old men began waving with their rifles.

"What are they tryin' to tell us?" Reese asked.

"That Smoke is waiting in the direction they're pointing," Richards said. "They're telling us to tangle with him—if we've got the sand in us to do so."

Potter did some fast counting. Out of what was once a hundred and fifty men, only nineteen remained, including himself. "Hell, boys! He's only one man. There's nineteen of us!"

"There was about this many over at that minin' camp, too," Britt said. "They couldn't stop him."

"Well," Kelly said. " 'Way I see it is this: we either fight ten of them ringtailed-tooters, or we fight Smoke."

"I'll take Smoke," Howard said. But he wasn't all that thrilled with the choices offered him.

The mountain men began moving, closing the circle. The gunhands turned their horses and moved out, allowing themselves to be pushed toward the west.

"They're pushing us toward Slate," Williams said. "The ghost town."

Richards smiled at Smoke's choice of a showdown spot.

As the old ghost town appeared on the horizon, located on the flats between the Lemhi River and the Beaverhead Range, Turkel's buddy, Harris, reined up and pointed. "Goddamn place is full of people!"

"Miners," Brown said. "They come to see the show. Drinking and betting. Them old mountain men spread the word."

"Just like it was at the camp on the Uncompahgre," Richards said with a grunt.* "Check your weapons.

*The Last Mountain Man.

Stuff your pockets full of extra shells. I'm going back to talk with Preacher. I want to see how this deal is going down."

Richards rode back to the mountain men, riding with one hand in the air.

"That there's far enuff," Lobo said. "Speak your piece."

"We win this fight, do we have to fight you men too?"

"No," Preacher said quickly. "My boy Smoke done laid down the rules."

His *boy*! Richards thought. Jesus God. "We win, do we get to stay in this part of the country?"

"If'n you win," Preacher said, "you leave with what you got on your backs. If'n you win, we pass the word, and here 'tis: if'n you or any of your people ever come west of Kansas, you dead meat. That clear?"

"You're a hard old man, Preacher."

"You wanna see jist how hard?" Preacher challenged.

"No," Richards said, shaking his head. "We'll take our chances with Smoke."

"You would be better off taking your chances with us," Audie suggested.

Richards looked at Nighthawk. "What do you have to say about it?"

"Ummm."

Richards looked pained.

"That means haul your ass back to your friends," Phew said.

Richards trotted his horse back to what was left of his band. He told them the rules.

Britt looked up the hill toward a old falling-down store. "There he is."

Smoke stood alone on the old curled-up and rotted boardwalk. The men could see his twin .44s belted around his waist. He held a Henry repeating rifle in his right hand, a double-barreled express gun in his left hand. Smoke ducked into the building, leaving only a slight bit of dust to signal where he once stood.

"Two groups of six," Richards said, "one group of three, one group of four. Britt, take your group in from the rear. Turkel, take your boys in from the east. Reese, take your people in from the west. I'll take my people in from this direction. Move out."

Smoke had removed his spurs, hanging them on the saddlehorn of Drifter. As soon as he ducked out of sight, he had run from the store down the hill, staying in the alley. He stashed the express gun on one side of the street in an old store, his rifle across the street. He met Skinny Davis first, in the gloom of what had once been a saloon.

"Draw!" Davis hissed.

Smoke put two holes in his chest before Davis could cock his .44s.

"In Pat's Saloon!" someone shouted.

Williams jumped through an open glassless window of the saloon. Just as his boots hit the old-warped floor, Smoke shot him, the .44 slug knocking the gunslick back out the window to the boardwalk. Williams was hurt, but not out of it yet. He crawled along the side of the building, one arm broken and dangling, useless.

"Smoke Jensen!" Cross called. "You ain't got the sand to face me!"

"That's one way of putting it," Smoke muttered, taking careful aim and shooting the outlaw. The lead struck him in the stomach, doubling him over and

183

dropping him to the weed-grown and dusty street.

The miners had hightailed it to the ridges surrounding the town. There they sat, drinking and betting and cheering. The mountain men stood and squatted and sat on the opposite ridge, watching.

A bullet dug a trench along the wood, sending splinters flying, a few of them striking Smoke's face, stinging and bringing a few drops of blood.

He ran out the back of the saloon and came face to face with Simpson, the gunhawk having both hands filled with .44.

Smoke pulled the trigger on his own .44s, the double hammer-blows of lead taking Simpson in the lower chest, slamming him to the ground, dying.

Quickly reloading, Smoke grabbed up Simpson's guns and tucked them behind his gunbelt. He ran down the alley. The last of Richards's gunslicks stepped out of a gaping doorway just as Smoke cut to his right, jumping through an open window. A bullet burned Smoke's shoulder. Spinning, he fired both Colts, one bullet striking Martin in the throat, the second taking the gunnie just above the nose, almost tearing off the upper part of the man's face.

Smoke caught a glimpse of someone running. He dropped to one knee and fired. His slug shattered the hip of Rogers, sending the big man sprawling in the dirt, howling and cursing. Reese spurred his horse and charged the building where Smoke was crouched. He smashed his horse's shoulder against the old door and thundered in. The horse, wild-eyed and scared witless, lost its footing and fell, pinning Reese to the floor, crushing the man's stomach and chest. Reese howled in agony as blood filled his mouth and darkness clouded his eyes.

Smoke left the dying man and ran out the side door. "Get him, Turkel!" Brown screamed.

Smoke glanced up. Turkel was on the roof of an old building, a rifle in his hand. Smoke flattened against a building as Turkel pulled the trigger, the slug plowing up dirt at Smoke's feet. Smoke snapped off a shot, getting lucky as the bullet hit the gunhand in the chest. Turkel dropped the rifle and fell to the street, crashing through an awning. He did not move.

A bullet removed a small part of Smoke's right upper ear; blood poured down the side of his face. He ran to where he had hid the shotgun, grabbing it up and cocking it, leveling it just as the doorway filled with men.

Firing both barrels, Smoke cleared the doorway of all living things, including Britt, Harris, and Smith, the buckshot knocking the men clear off the rotting boardwalk, dead and dying in the street.

"Goddamn you, Jensen!" Brown screamed in rage, stepping out into the street.

Smoke dropped the shotgun and picked up a bloody rifle from the doorway. He shot Brown in the stomach. Brown howled and dropped to the street, both hands holding his stomach.

Rogers leveled a pistol and fired, the bullet ricocheting off a support post, part of the lead striking Smoke's left leg, dropping him to the boardwalk. Smoke ended Rogers's career with a single shot to the head.

White-hot pain lanced through Smoke's side as Williams shot him from behind. Smoke fell off the boardwalk, turning as he fell. He fired twice, the lead taking Williams in the neck, almost tearing the man's head off.

Ducking back inside, grabbing up a fallen shotgun with blood on the barrel, Smoke checked the shotgun, then checked his wounds. Bleeding, but not serious. Williams's slug had gone through the fleshy part of the side. Using the point of his knife, Smoke picked out the tiny piece of lead from Rogers's gun and tied a bandana around the slight wound. He slipped further into the darkness of the building as spurs jingled in the alley to the rear of the old store. Smoke jacked back both hammers on the coach gun. He waited.

The spurs jingled once more. Smoke followed the sound with the twin barrels of the express gun. Carefully, silently, he slipped across the rat-droppings-littered floor to the wall that fronted the alley. He could hear breathing directly in front of him.

He pulled both triggers, the charge blowing a bucket-sized hole in the old pine wall.

The gunslick was blown clear across the alley, hurled against an outhouse. The outhouse collapsed, the gunhand falling into the pit.

Silently, Smoke reloaded the shotgun, then reloaded his own .44s and the ones taken from the dead gunnie. He listened as Fenerty called for his buddies.

There was no reply.

Fenerty was the last gunhawk left.

Smoke located the voice. Just across the street in a falling-down old building. Laying aside the shotgun, he picked up a rifle and emptied the magazine into the storefront. Fenerty came staggering out, shot in the chest and belly. He died face down in the littered street.

"All right, you bastards!" Smoke yelled to Richards, Potter, and Stratton. "Holster your guns and step out into the street. Face me, if you've got the nerve."

The sharp odor of sweat mingled with blood and gunsmoke filled the still summer air as four men stepped out into the bloody dusty street.

Richards, Potter, and Stratton stood at one end of the block. A tall, bloody figure stood at the other. All their guns were in leather.

"You son of a bitch!" Stratton screamed, his voice as high-pitched as a woman. "You ruined it all." He clawed at his .44.

Smoke drew and fired before Stratton's pistol could clear leather. Potter grabbed for his pistol. Smoke shot him dead, then holstered his gun, waiting.

Richards had not moved. He stood with a faint smile on his lips, staring at Smoke.

"You ready to die?" Smoke asked the man.

"As ready as I'll ever be, I suppose," Richards replied. There was no fear in his voice. His hands appeared steady. "Janey gone?"

"Took your money and pulled out."

"Been a long run, hasn't it, Jensen?"

"It's just about over."

"What happens to all our holdings?"

"I don't care what happens to the mines. The miners can have them. I'm giving all your stock to decent, honest punchers and homesteaders."

A puzzled look spread over Richards' face. "I don't understand. You did . . . all *this*!" he waved his hand—"for nothing?"

Someone moaned, the sound painfully inching up the street.

"I did it for my pa, my brother, my wife, and my baby son."

"But it won't bring them back!"

"I know."

"I wish I had never heard the name Jensen."

"You'll never hear it again after this day, Richards."

"One way to find out," Richards said with a smile. He drew his Colt and fired. He was snake-quick, but hurried his shot, the lead digging up dirt at Smoke's feet.

Smoke shot him in the right shoulder, spinning the man around. Richards grabbed for his left-hand gun and Smoke fired again, the slug striking the man in the left side of his chest. He struggled to bring up his Colt. He managed to cock it before Smoke's third shot struck him in the belly. Richards sat down hard in the bloody, dusty street.

He opened his mouth to speak. He tasted blood on his tongue. The light began to fade around him. "You'll . . . meet . . ."

Smoke never found who he was supposed to meet. Richards toppled over on his side and died.

Smoke looked up at the ridge where the mountain men had gathered.

They were gone, leaving as silently as the wind.

24

After MacGregor filed his report with the commanding officer at the fort, the Army made only a cursory inspection of what was left of Bury, Idaho Territory, and the burned ranches around it.

Wanted posters were put out for the outlaw and murderer Buck West. MacGregor wrote the description of the man, thus insuring he would never be found.

A lot of small ranches sprang up around the area. Very prosperous little farms and ranchers. The ladies from the Pink House stayed. They all got married.

Sam married Becky.

The last anyone ever saw of Smoke Jensen and Sally Reynolds, the two of them were riding toward the mountains, toward the High Lonesome, leading two packhorses.

"You think we'll ever see them again?" Becky asked Sam.

Sam did not reply.

But as Nighthawk might have said, "Ummm."

BEST OF THE WEST
from Zebra Books

BROTHER WOLF   (1728, $2.95)
by Dan Parkinson
Only two men could help Lattimer run down the sheriff's killers—a stranger named Stillwell and an Apache who was as deadly with a Colt as he was with a knife. One of them would see justice done—from the muzzle of a six-gun.

CALAMITY TRAIL   (1663, $2.95)
by Dan Parkinson
Charles Henry Clayton fled to the west to make his fortune, get married and settle down to a peaceful life. But the situation demanded that he strap on a six-gun and ride toward a showdown of gunpowder and blood that would send him galloping off to either death or glory on the . . . *Calamity Trail*.

THUNDERLAND   (1991, $3.50)
by Dan Parkinson
Men were suddenly dying all around Jonathan, and he needed to know why—before he became the next bloody victim of the ancient sword that would shape the future of the Texas frontier.

APACHE GOLD   (1899, $2.95)
by Mark K. Roberts & Patrick E. Andrews
Chief Halcon burned with a fierce hatred for the pony soldiers that rode from Fort Dawson, and vowed to take the scalp of every round-eye in the territory. Sergeant O'Callan must ride to glory or death for peace on the new frontier.

OKLAHOMA SHOWDOWN   (1961, $2.25)
by Patrick E. Andrews
When Dace chose the code of lawman over an old friendship, he knew he might have to use his Colt .45 to back up his choice. Because a meeting between good friends who'd ended up on different sides of the law as sure to be one blazing hellfire.

Available wherever paperbacks are sold, or order direct from the Publisher. Send cover price plus 50¢ per copy for mailing and handling to Zebra Books, Dept. 1816, 475 Park Avenue South, New York, N.Y. 10016. Residents of New York, New Jersey and Pennsylvania must include sales tax. DO NOT SEND CASH.

VISIT THE WILD WEST
with Zebra Books

SPIRIT WARRIOR   (1795, $2.50)
by G. Clifton Wisler

The only settler to survive the savage Indian attack was a little boy. Although raised as a red man, every man was his enemy when the two worlds clashed—but he vowed no man would be his equal.

IRON HEART   (1736, $2.25)
by Walt Denver

Orphaned by an Indian raid, Ben vowed he'd never rest until he'd brought death to the Arapahoes. And it wasn't long before they came to fear the rider of vengeance they called . . . *Iron Heart.*

THE DEVIL'S BAND   (1903, $2.25)
by Robert McCaig

For Pinkerton detective Justin Lark, the next assignment was the most dangerous of his career. To save his beautiful young client's sisters and brother, he had to face the meanest collection of hardcases he had ever seen.

KANSAS BLOOD   (1775, $2.50)
by Jay Mitchell

The Barstow Gang put a bullet in Toby Markham, but they didn't kill him. And when the Barstow's threatened a young girl named Lonnie, Toby was finished with running and ready to start killing.

SAVAGE TRAIL   (1594, $2.25)
by James Persak

Bear Paw seemed like a harmless old Indian—until he stole the nine-year-old son of a wealthy rancher. In the weeks of brutal fighting the guns of the White Eyes would clash with the ancient power of the red man.